GENIE-ALOGY

A Novella

I0533094

H.B. Morris

Genie-alogy

a novella

H.B. Morris

978-0-9570745-7-6

Published by Bronwyn Editions in the United Kingdom 2015
http://www.bronwyneditions.co.uk

Cover design: Esther Kezia Harding

Printed by Lightning Source UK 2015

This book has been ghost-written and republished under a pseudonym

PROLOGUE

'I'll meet you at the old trafford,' she had said.

Nathan Levy arrived in good time, despite taking an unintended detour through Salford Quays. He had "borrowed" his father's Audi A5, thinking it would look better to her than his battered Ford Focus. As a Manchester City fan he had never actually been to the enemy stadium before, just glimpsed the evil edifice from way off while driving on the motorway. The car-park he pulled into seemed to be the right one, empty in July except for a few coaches, one of which was disgorging African tourists in a long stream of multi-coloured dresses, head scarves and aimed cameras.

Nathan stepped out into a lovely, breezy day and looked at the Sir Alex Ferguson stand high above him. A wry smile came to his face – of all places, their first meeting had to be "the old trafford". He had corrected her at first, but when she kept on referring to it that way, he decided it was how it would be for him too. Her coach was on the way up from London, stopping at the ground first, before it carried on to Liverpool, for Anfield stadium and the Beatles experience.

He turned slowly 360 degrees to take in the panorama of Trafford Park industrial estate and the glass skyscrapers of the Quays. Hitching his bag and locking his car he strolled after the Africans, up a ramp over a canal, which was a surprise to him, then down towards the entrance to the gift shop and the museum. There were other solitary people moving about, so he played the role of lingering tourist. His phone buzzed in his back pocket; on inspection she was texting to say she was close.

He drifted back over the ramp. Another coach let out a stream of

Asian tourists, but they looked Japanese – he was waiting for Indonesian. He leant against the Audi. He was extraordinarily happy. Another text told him she was desperate for a pee, so would be running straight in when they arrived.

Within two minutes another coach pulled in. She was first off, looking around for him. So adorable. Jet black hair blowing in the breeze. Small and cute, wearing her nerdy glasses. She hugged a maroon cardigan around herself and started walking in her skinny jeans and what looked like slippers. She saw him, smiled and waved. He waved back, watching her move towards the ramp.

Next off the coach was the Tour Guide, immediately recognisable to him as his Uncle Simon, although he had not seen him since he was fourteen, four years ago. Aunt Nadya stepped off next. She must have been a foot shorter than her husband, and dressed in traditional white Indonesian garb. Simon Levy ran a tourism firm in Jakarta, Indonesia, usually taking business clients all over Asia. Coming to Europe was unusual to him. That's why his daughter, Kezia, had tagged along. She had volunteered to help with the clients, and being half-English, after all, it was time to see her other home, while now at an age, seventeen, to be able to enjoy it.

Nathan walked over and made his presence known to his relatives. Simon's face lit up as he recognised his brother's son and took him into an embrace. Nadya smiled warmly and hugged him too.

'Kezia's run in to the loo,' said Simon.

'I know, I saw her. How's the trip working out, Uncle Simon?'

'Everything's going a treat. London was wonderful. We can't wait to see the family next week.'

'They're excited too. Listen, I'll let you care for your clients. I'll go and chase Kezia.'

The group were disembarking. One or two were already wearing the red United shirts. Nathan got a kiss on the cheek from Auntie Nadya, then stepped out of the way. He moved ahead of everyone and went over the ramp again. Over the club threshold he went. The foyer was quite busy. He just sat inside for a while watching the excited fans milling about. Then he decided to go in search of Kezia. A member of staff gave him directions to the toilets, which were upstairs, so he took the lift. Immediately on stepping out he bumped into cousin Kezia and she threw herself into his arms. The emotions of that moment would stay with Nathan for the rest of his life. There were a lot of people present, so they could not express their delight right then and there. She indicated for them to go back down.

She wouldn't ride the lift with him, not because she was scared of lifts, but due to the fact that her parents were unaware of the relationship that had grown between the two of them, via the internet, over the last six months. He stepped out in the foyer. She came down the stairs, nervously grinning. He followed her outside. There was no sign of the Indonesian party, and for a moment they didn't know where to go, with her twice touching his forearm, as if checking that he was really, truly there. They drifted a little way underneath the stand and moved behind a booth of some kind. Once they were hidden from everyone but a few wandering passers-by they came back together. She was smaller than him, quite beautifully delicate. He caressed her small jaw. Touched her hair. Her eyes found his over her glasses. They kissed for the first time, awkward but perfect. They held each other and felt all the love and their internet naughtiness flood through them, and they just knew that they had to be together for the rest of their lives.

On the walk to the Audi it was hard to keep their hands off each other. While the tour continued on to Liverpool and then Edinburgh, Kezia was to stay with her relatives, rejoining during the overnight stop in Manchester (when both families were coming together), before the Cotswolds and the flight home from Heathrow. They had said goodbye to her parents in the gift shop. The fact that Nathan's parents were currently on a coach trip round the Lincolnshire Wolds was not mentioned. Nathan and Kezia had four glorious days alone together. In the car, he had to look down a little bit to her, so sweet, sitting there in the passenger seat.

'Are you all right?' he asked.

She nodded. 'I love you.'

'I love you too.'

As he drove away she put her hand on his thigh.

ONE

Seven years later

Nathan Levy had just spent the best part of two hours making love to the sexiest woman imaginable – Mrs Jodie O'Neil. Illicit daylight seeped its way through the closed blinds of her bedroom window.

Nathan propped himself up on an elbow and traversed the fingers of his right hand slowly down through the firm gap between her breasts – he was still being most attentive, perhaps angling for a complimentary appraisal of his efforts.

Mrs O'Neil, maybe four or five years older than his twenty-five, kept her thoughts to herself. She ran a hand through her luscious black hair, checking the time on her twisted wristwatch. Nathan thought she could have made that glance at the watch a little less obvious, but never mind. He scanned her beautiful face, but she was clearly not going to say anything.

'What are you thinking?' he had to ask.

'I'm thinking, I'd like to meet your brother.'

Nathan laughed. To make conversation earlier, he had told her about his older brother's latest project. Zac Levy was a writer who published novels on places like Kindle. He'd been struggling to find a suitable image for his independent publisher to incorporate into the cover artwork, so had dug out old photo's of ex-girlfriends. He chose one of a girl he'd not seen for about seven years: a real beauty who he'd never really got over and, because his publisher said he needed permission to use it, had written to her setting out his plans. Apparently, she had been flattered and gave him the go ahead. Now Zac was getting malicious phone calls at four o'clock in the morning and the girl's current boyfriend was threatening to break his legs.

'It's such a romantic gesture,' sighed Mrs O'Neil. 'No-one's ever done anything like that for me. Do you remember the girl?'

Nathan grinned. 'Not really. I wasn't into older women back then.'

Mrs O'Neil tutted and removed herself from the bed. She slipped on a tee-shirt and looked out to the street below. Nathan marvelled at her smooth legs.

'Mrs O'Neil, come back to bed.'

'Nathan, there's a man knocking on your front door.'

'Maybe your husband has hired a private detective.'

'Well, if he has, he's hired the worst private detective in the world.'

Nathan sat up, pulled on his jeans and joined her at the window, hugging her from behind. 'Babe, that's a Jehovah's Witness down there.'

'Jehovah's Witnesses don't show up in a black Maserati.'

Nathan pretended to quiver. 'Ooh, I love a woman who knows her cars.'

'Are you going to see what he wants?'

'You're joking, aren't you?'

Nathan finished dressing.

'Are you running off on me?' asked Mrs O'Neil, pretending to be bothered.

'Tell me I was wonderful.'

'You were wonderful.'

He kissed her. 'Text me, next time you're free.'

She waved him off and he was away down the stairs.

His South Manchester street no longer had a Jehovah's Witness or a Maserati on it, but he did bump into an old friend, who went by the name of Elvis, a wild-eyed, curly-haired youth.

'Nathan, my man.' Elvis looked left and right, as if he were conducting a drugs deal. 'Come. Ale house.'

Nathan draped an arm over Elvis's shoulders. 'Can't, mate. I'm going to grab a sandwich, then I'm off to work.' They had no choice but to follow a trail of litter along the pavement towards a bakery on the corner. 'What have you been up to? I heard you got arrested.'

'I'll tell you the truth, I was coming out of a pub with the lads, and was having a piss in a bush. Felt this tap on the shoulder. This Dibble asks, "What are you doing?" Having a piss, what do you think I'm doing? "Have you finished?" Yes. "Right, you're under arrest for indecent exposure." I said, you're having a fucking laugh, aren't you? They stuck me in the back of their car, handcuffed. Fucking *handcuffed*.'

Nathan began to crack up with laughter.

'What do you think I'm gonna do? I ask. Attack you with my dick? They took me back to the station and stood me in front of the desk sergeant. "What's the charge?" he asks. "Indecent exposure."' Nathan was crying with laughter. 'I tell you, I couldn't believe it. I was having a piss, I protested. I asked the desk sergeant if he'd ever had a piss in a bush and he said no. He stood there and said no. Then they locked me in a cell for five hours, before letting me go.'

Nathan indicated the bakery. 'I gotta make a move, mate.'

'Yeah, go on. I'll see you soon.'

Nathan and Elvis connected fists in parting. Then Elvis saw one of the staff members through the bakery window and cringed his face away.

'What's up?' asked Nathan.

'That girl there, serving behind the counter. She was at a fireworks party, last Bonfire Night. She looked cold, so I offered her my coat. Unfortunately the sleeve she put her hand in happened to be tucked down the front of my pants. She gave me a right slap. I still intend to bang her, though.'

Both men laughed. Nathan watched his friend saunter off, before entering the shop.

He ordered two sausage rolls from a different assistant, from

Sullen Sally in the hairnet. He paid the extortionate price. Suddenly fatigued from his time with Mrs O'Neil, he found a wall to sit on, watching the world go by as he ate. He saw a local woman who he knew vaguely, pushing her baby in its pushchair while her other child toddled along behind. The child was constantly looking up for mummy's attention, but mummy was totally engrossed in her phone. All the way from Mallon street to George Crescent, the length of Nathan's lunch, the child was ignored. Nathan owned a cell phone too, but for some unknown reason he disliked the way the world was going as far as technology was concerned. He wondered what would happen if there were no more electricity for these texting cretins. He felt like giving the woman a slap, telling her to care more for her daughter, but decided better of it.

He walked back home to his rented little box of a house, on a street of dozens of similar, rented little boxes of houses, and took a shower. After that he phoned his mechanic friend to see how the work on his Audi A3 was going – *soon, soon, mate* he was assured. Then he dressed and thought about walking to work, which wasn't far, to one of the airport hotels where he was employed as a bartender. But that would mean negotiating the tram extension road works that apparently would be taking six years to complete. Six years! Instead, he walked round the corner to the flat of one of his girlfriends and borrowed her car.

Halfway along Ringway road, with the airport perimeter fence on his left, a massive Emirates jet took off. Nathan craned his neck to watch it go. All his life he'd lived in that area, and he was yet to fly out of Manchester airport.

***

To look at facially, Professor Steven Pyle, at sixty years of age, appeared quite sane. If you panned out to include his multi-coloured ski gear, complete with goggles and bobble hat, and put him on a dry ski slope in the middle of Surrey in May, well...

He was framed against the clear blue. Staff fussed around him. A man called Jackson West, a professional photographer, stood taking his picture, while alongside him was Lucy West, freelance reporter with pen and pad paused in mid-air as if she no longer knew what to write. Jackson and Lucy were not related – divorced, actually, having been that rare thing of two people with the same surname who got married. They were both in their early twenties – so at least they could blame their age for the break-up. They were amicable, still liked each other and continued to work together.

'Lucy,' said Pyle, 'forgive me, I forgot to ask, how are your quarters here? They are up to scratch, I trust?'

In her peripheral vision, Lucy could see the wing of Pyle's country pile in which she and Jackson were temporarily housed.

'They're excellent, sir,' she said. 'Thank you.'

Lucy glanced at Jackson, who carried an expression which seemed to say "well don't worry about me, then, professor".

'Professor Pyle,' continued Lucy, 'can I have your initial reaction to being short-listed for the Nobel prize, for your work in the fields of genetics and DNA?'

Pyle smiled – good teeth, probably not original. Then he hit his ski poles together as if to remove real snow.

'Ah, now, listen. When I was younger I was very good at snooker – stay with me, Lucy, I can see you drifting away there. I won a lot of amateur tournaments. But, show me the money. Show me the money! I always left the trophies in the toilet. I didn't mean to be rude, but I just didn't want them. I need the feeling of accomplishment within myself, and the cash, not trophies.'

'I see.'

'I didn't need other people telling me how great I am. But I've mellowed with age. I may just show up, if they really want me.'

'Right you are.'

'I'm going now. You will be following me down, won't you, dear?'

Lucy paused, then nodded vigorously. 'Right behind you, Professor.'

Pyle, helped by a member of staff, hopped his skis onto the tracks at the top of the slope and pushed off. Lucy and Jackson, through his clicking camera lens, watched him go, then looked at each other.

Lucy shook her head. 'God help us, Jackson. Where's the bloody lift?'

Pyle shot off the end of the dry slope, completely out of control. Twenty feet from the ground, and certain death, he was suddenly caught in a cushion of air. The invisible safety net slowly subsided to allow Pyle to come down to earth, exhilarated, smiling at yet more aides who rushed to his assistance.

In the kitchen of the Pyle residence, Pringle, the butler, sat drinking tea and eating chocolate digestive biscuits in the company of the cook, Angela. His stripy waistcoat lay open at his hips and his shoes were off – very much a Downstairs moment of rest and relaxation.

'Get it out, then,' prompted Angela, sitting herself down beside him. Her eyes were wide and attentive; she loved the man's visits to her kitchen.

Half-reluctantly, Pringle brought an envelope up from beneath the table.

'You'll have to open it, Angela. I'm far too nervous.'

Angela took the manila envelope from him, ripped it open and a pale green document slipped out. 'Shall I read it aloud?'

'Please do.'

'What have we here, then? Frank Pringle... Is that the fellow you're looking for?'

'Yes, that's great-grandfather Frank.'

'Died April 30th 1933, Nell Lane, Withington...'

'Workhouse.'

'Is it?'

'Chorlton Union Workhouse, Manchester. Go on, please.'

'Err, there's his name, male, 33 years old, of 25 Silk Street, Newton Heath, a firelighter manufacturer. Cause of death... pneumonia accelerated by chronic alcoholism. Then, coroner's signature.'

Pringle digested the news solemnly. Angela patted his hand. Behind them, through a window, a tiny shape came flying off the ski slope.

TWO

Nathan Levy had just finished his bartender shift in the Manchester Airport hotel where he worked. With a wave to colleagues, and a hug from the fantastically nubile barmaid, Beverley, he exited through an open fire door and made off across the car-park. He was heckled by some rough, but friendly chambermaids at the gates to Housekeeping.

'Going already?' they called, good-naturedly. 'Part-timer, you.'

'Hey,' he threw back, 'I was standing in for sick-boy Carl. I've earned Brownie points today.'

'You crawler.'

They all waved as he walked on. What a wonderful late afternoon, Nathan thought, partly wasted by being trapped indoors; he gave his face up to the sun, until he heard his name being called. It was Frank, a fellow bartender, just arriving. The older man walked towards Nathan with a pronounced limp.

'What have you done to yourself?' asked Nathan, grinning.

'I just turned quick and my lower back went. It was agony. I was on the floor for about half an hour. People just stepped over me.'

'Where were you, in the street?'

'No, my front room.'

Nathan laughed, then started to copy the man. 'You should get a job at one of those car-parks in town. The attendant always has a limp, you know, when he comes over shouting a warning, "Ee-ar, mate, you can't park there!"'

Frank shared the joke and they went their separate ways with slaps on the shoulders.

'Take it easy, Frank.'

Then Nathan heard his name called again. A man in a sharp suit, holding a manila envelope, stood beside a black Maserati.

'Mr Nathan Levy? My name's Damon Julius. I've been charged with delivering this...'

'No, mate!' Nathan's hands were up flamboyantly. He laughed. 'It's a summons, isn't it? I know it's a summons.'

Nathan got quickly into a little Fiat Cinquecento with ludicrously big alloy wheels. Damon Julius made no further attempt to continue the conversation. Nathan briefly got back out of the Fiat, a little embarrassed with his mode of transport.

'This car's not mine, by the way. It's the girlfriend's.'

Damon Julius just smiled.

***

Middle-aged, plain, anonymous Carla Terry still managed to stop traffic in Bexleyheath, south east London. She did it with her fluorescent coat and big Stop! Children! lollipop. She was well into her shift one afternoon when a regular mother with children went by.

'Hello, Carla.'

'Oh, hello, Jean. How are you, love?'

'Have you got any further with your family tree?'

'All done, I think, apart from the impossible ones to find. I'm going round in circles now trying to gather little snippets of information about the ones I've got.'

'I wish I was as dedicated as you. I've finally got my grandparents names and I'm delighted with that.'

Carla guided them over the road. 'It's good fun, though, isn't it?'

'It is, yes. I'll see you tomorrow.'

'No doubt you will. Cheerio.'

Carla lingered around for a little while, helping a few late stragglers. She smiled at some nice children and scowled at a few impatient drivers. Finally she decided that would do for the day. She put her lollipop in its regular place behind a low wall and began to head home.

Another man in a dark suit stepped from another black Maserati.

'Mrs Terry? Hello, my name's Warren Mansergh. Have you got a moment? I have an envelope for you.'

'Have you, my dear? How very nice. What is it, young man?'

'Open it, Mrs Terry. You'll be pleasantly surprised.'

Carla did open the envelope and was, indeed, pleasantly surprised.

***

In San Diego, California, Dr Jada Mountfield was on duty at the Sharp Chula Vista Medical Centre. She had just finished stapling the split ear of a young black boy, and stood back to assess her work.

'I always thought soccer was a dangerous game,' she said to the boy's mother, with a smile. Then to the boy, 'All done. I was in England recently. They call soccer football over there.'

The boy rolled his eyes and nodded that he knew that fact already. Jada and the boy's mother laughed as they led him out. A nurse took over proceedings and Jada stepped into the front office, where only a few patients remained. She felt a little tired – it had been a busy day. She touched her eyes with the back of her wrist and smiled at an approaching male colleague.

'Jada, you get off home,' said Dr Kahn, 'I'll finish up here.'

'Michael, you're a sweetheart. Pete's picking me up. We're going camping for the weekend.'

Jada Mountfield was a beautiful twenty-five-year-old of mixed race, with a glowing complexion and full, sexy lips. Dr Kahn managed to hide his feelings that he would have liked to be under canvas with her himself for a whole week.

Jada went to the staff locker room, changed clothes, and called her boyfriend on his cell phone. He said he was already on his way,

16

so she collected up her possessions and went to wait out front.

This was her first proper position since qualifying as a doctor. The plan had been to work in her home state of Illinois, but when her best friend went and stole her boyfriend, she had wanted to get as far away as possible without getting her feet wet. She loved her adoptive San Diego, probably because she had met her Pete soon after arriving, and that helped her settle in. Pete, an African-American, was a fireman, a little younger than her, with the build of a WWF wrestler. He loved to surf, and was starting to win her round to perhaps accepting lessons from him – and because of the *love thing* she had changed her mind that the ocean only belonged to the sharks.

Pete's black SUV pulled in. She had expected the roof rack to be already loaded, but it was clearly empty, and Pete's apologetic expression as he jumped down made it obvious that the trip was off. She looked at him with a wry grin as he jogged across the car park and picked her up into a hug as if she weighed nothing – which she virtually did.

'What's happened?' she asked.

'A couple of the guys, the Lomax brothers, had a bereavement. Their father.' He put her down on her feet. 'I agreed to work this weekend.'

'Oh, that's so sad. I'm sorry to hear that. Well, never mind about going away. We'll do it some other time.'

'I've still got a few hours, baby. Maybe we could...'

'Maybe we could go eat, Pete. I'm starving.'

'That's what I meant. Let's go eat.'

THREE

Nathan drove to the little Cheshire village of Gatley, south of Manchester, and parked up the Cinquecento on the high street.

He walked into a wine bar where he knew his other girlfriend, Emma, would be and stopped in his tracks. He was having a revelation – almost everybody standing in the posh establishment was staring at their mobile device. It was actually frightening, like a bad sci-fi movie. Nathan was in no way so permanently attached to his own phone. He moved through the crowds until he found Emma with her friends, sitting in the leather sofa section and, of course, they all had their mobiles in front of their faces. He had known what she was like when he got with her the previous summer. He had made a joke about her falling down a hole because she walked along, constantly texting, and how the NHS would soon be overwhelmed by girls with broken noses. Once or twice he even had to remove the device from her hand prior to lovemaking, and occasionally felt, in the height of passion, that she had urges towards where it sat on the bedside cabinet.

Emma stood up, he thought to give him a romantic welcome, but she only wanted to go to the toilet, so he settled for a peck on his cheek and followed her through to the corridor where the Ladies was.

'Shall I hold the phone?' he asked, cheekily, as she went through the door.

'Don't be silly.'

When she came out, thankfully the phone was off, and they kissed up against a wall.

'I've no time for you,' she said.

'Oh, thanks.'

'You remember, us girls are going to see *One Direction*.'

'I know. It's tragic. When you're forty you'll be embarrassed by the very memory. I just wanted to grab five minutes with you, that's all.'

Emma was brunette, about five foot two, with dark-rimmed, intellectual glasses, quite a posh girl, who had bailed on university because there was always a place for her in the family property rental empire. Daddy had given her a house in nearby Cheadle.

'Will you come round tomorrow?' she asked. 'I'll do brunch, then you can do me.'

'I'll see if I can fit you in.'

She took his hand and led him back to the bar. It was Emma's friend, Hannah, who gave him the big hug and kiss, as she took her turn going to the Ladies.

'Nathan, will you take me, as well?' she asked.

Nathan slapped her bottom. 'Get on with you, you little minx.'

He sat down, suddenly wondering if Emma was bothered by his flirtation with Hannah – but Emma was on her phone, texting.

***

'Don't take my fucking car without asking me!'

Nathan completed the action of closing the door to the flat of his other girlfriend and went in search of her dulcet tones.

'Rachel, darling, it's me.'

She was in the tiny lounge, painting her toenails near to the open French windows. There came the sound of a faulty lawnmower somewhere below the window.

'Don't give me that. I had to get the bus today,' continued Rachel Ikin.

'My car will be out of the garage tomorrow,' he assured her.

'And I wish that knobhead would fix his lawnmower. The noise is getting right on my tits.'

The noise was drowned out by the sound of a plane taking off from the airport. Nathan waited for the sound of the aircraft to fade.

'Are we still planning on going to Sheffield?' he asked.

'Yeah, we are. We'll be going to a club, by the way. Don't be shocked by my girlfriends.' Rachel stood up to the window and screamed, 'Oi! Knobhead! Pack that racket in!'

She nonchalantly sat back down and began talking, while another loud plane took off. It amused Nathan that she was oblivious to the greater noise pollution. Smiling at her, he leant down to kiss her offered up puckered lips.

The Sheffield thing was through the college Rachel attended until last year. She was not a Yorkshire lass. She was born and bred Benchill, Wythenshawe, which, basically, meant she was a bit rough. But she was so cute – jet black hair, small in stature and all soft skin to cuddle up to. Nathan didn't think he loved her, he just liked her very much. He didn't love anything definitely, except his mother, he supposed. Everything to do with life was like that for Nathan Levy; stress free, go the easiest way, leave all the deep thinking to brother Zac and his novels that sold in their... dozens.

'Where are we eating tonight?' asked Rachel.

'I was thinking of that sofa over there. Unless you've been paid early.'

'I should find a man who looks after me better.'

'Good luck with that.'

***

Carla Terry arrived home to her scruffy terraced house in Bexleyheath, with music that she could neither stand nor understand blaring from a neighbour's bedroom window. As she let herself in, she could see through to where her husband sat at the kitchen table.

'It's me,' she called. 'I have something to tell you.'

Mr Terry began his work at five o'clock in the morning, so ate his tea early. He was overweight, uncouth, and stuffing his face with sausage and mash when Carla came into the kitchen, removing her coat and hanging it up.

'Carla, wait 'til I tell you about my day. It's unbelievable.'

'Something has happened...'

'Me and John had to clear a woman's house in Peckham. The worst we've ever done. She's not cleaned up, washed a pot, taken out any rubbish in thirty years. The place stank. Two dead cats under the bed where she sleeps. Can you believe that? Shit up the kitchen wall. John couldn't keep his breakfast down. But we got it clear in the end.'

Carla washed her hands and started to think about what she could do for her own tea.

'What were you saying, Carla?'

'Oh, nothing. My mother has invited me down to Margate next week. I might stay over for several days.'

'Okay. I'll survive. I'll get a curry after the Spurs match.'

Carla left the kitchen to go upstairs, hiding Warren Mansergh's letter in her hand.

***

Jada met up with two friends from work, Harmonee and Tracy, at Chili's Grill and Bar on North Harbor Drive, one of their favourite places to hang out. Harmonee, a bubbly, petite, black woman, worked on the hospital reception desk, while Tracy was a certified nursing assistant. The three of them had clicked immediately and had the same sense of humour.

Jada had explained why she was not away for the weekend and Harmonee had instructed her to dump Pete, forthwith, so she could go out with him herself. They giggled over their nachos and cokes.

Tracy was a nineteen-year-old Hispanic girl, the only one

currently not dating, so perhaps that had something to do with her spotting the handsome man, watching them from his own table nearby. Harmonee checked him out, as did Jada, only a little less obviously. The man smiled.

'He's sat on his own,' said Jada. 'That's interesting. Maybe he's a businessman, waiting for a client to show up.'

'I don't care what he is,' said Harmonee, giggling, 'but he's coming over.'

The man wore a dark suit and carried a friendly expression on his face. Tracy was nearest, so she got his hand resting on the top of her chair, causing her to pull an embarrassed girly face at her friends.

'Ladies,' smiled the man, 'would you allow me to buy you all a drink?'

Jada picked up on the English accent, not so much because she had recently holidayed there, but because it was so clipped and proper, as if he were educated at Eton and Cambridge.

Harmonee cheerily accepted for them all, of course, and made him pull up a chair. He sat near to Jada.

'Where are you from, honey?' asked Harmonee.

The man half-gestured, 'I'm from over there.'

Harmonee screamed her shrill laugh. Tracy and Jada smiled.

Jada said, 'Let me introduce us. Harmonee, there. Tracy. And I'm Jada.'

'My name's Nigel. Nigel Bissett. And, Harmonee, to answer your question, I'm from Cheltenham in England. I'm so sorry for staring. This is my first time in California, and I was just enjoying the local sights.'

'No need to apologise,' said Harmonee.

The girls' main meals arrived. As Jada made room on the table for her Buffalo Chicken Ranch sandwich, she was aware that Nigel Bissett seemed to be most interested in her. Harmonee was ordering various margaritas from the waitress.

'Jada?' asked Nigel, 'Do you mind if I bring my meal over to your table?'

'No, not at all.'

She watched him visit his table and carry his plates and a few document folders back to them. He was certainly an attractive man – a suave Englishman. But she was not even remotely interested. She had her Pete.

Nigel settled himself down. He looked hard at Jada, then he seemed to check himself, and gave more attention to Harmonee and Tracy.

Nigel proved to be fun company and added to their conversations. He gave them some business gobbledegook about why he was in San Diego, but none of the girls pressed him on the matter. Jada did note that Nigel didn't once ask what any of them did for a living. Jada, of course, told Nigel of her recent visit to England.

'Oh, how fascinating,' he said. 'I hope you didn't just do the tourist thing.'

'No. I was in Wolverhampton and Stoke mostly.'

'Good grief, that is off the beaten track.'

Over dessert, it was as if they had known Nigel for years. His fascination with Jada seemed to have waned, and Tracy had become the apple of his eye. Harmonee organised the girls' bill. Nigel wanted to pick up the whole tab.

'You can't do that,' said Jada, quite adamant.

'Oh, please,' said Nigel. 'I insist. It's been such fun.'

While Jada and Harmonee conferred on the offer (Harmonee always liked a freebie), Tracy took her chance, asking, 'Nigel, how long are you in San Diego for?'

'A few more days. Maybe a week.'

'Would you like to do something? I mean, go out somewhere.'

'Tracy, I'd be honoured. Perhaps, we could go for a drink now?'

Tracy blushed. 'Sure.'

While Nigel settled the bill, Harmonee and Tracy went to powder their noses. Nigel turned to Jada. 'Jada, don't be alarmed. I've actually come to San Diego to see you.'

Jada was alarmed. 'What?'

'Here.' Nigel offered her an envelope.

Jada accepted the envelope, opened it and scanned its contents. Delight flooded across her face, but she managed to control herself by the time she saw her friends approaching.

'Don't respond now,' said Nigel, smiling. 'Take a couple of days to let it sink in. My number's in the envelope.'

Jada could only nod her head. Nigel jumped up to meet the excited Tracy, taking hold of her hands.

'Right, then, Tracy,' he said. 'I'm completely at your command, young lady.'

Tracy just blushed and giggled.

FOUR

There are two attractions at the Pyle residence which can been seen above the conifer trees from the villages just outside the grounds: the ski-slope and also the man's very own roller-coaster. Lucy and Jackson took a ride on it, in the front carriage, the only passengers. As it started to ascend for the first time, Lucy asked, 'Jackson, shall we sack this?'

'It's a bit late, girl, we're strapped in.'

'No, I mean this assignment.'

'You're joking, it's paint-balling this afternoon.'

'I'll ring the office. Beg to be pulled off it. I mean, what's going on? Three people win a lottery and get a short holiday here. It's not exactly Willy Wonka.'

'I don't know, Lucy. This Pyle's eccentric enough to have something up his sleeve. Maybe they've all got an illness and he's going to cure them with some new procedure. That'll be worth our time.'

'I hope you're right. Jackson, I hate roller-coasters.'

'Why come on it, then?'

'It was either this or a game of tennis with Pyle. Here we go!'

The coaster went over the top and thundered down the other side.

At one stage on the ride, if Lucy and Jackson had not been upside down, they would have been able to see over the 17th century part of the Surrey mansion to a brand new high-tech addition tacked onto the side. Here was Professor Pyle's laboratory, where he stood in conversation with his assistant, Dr Charles Robinson, a man in his fifties who had all the qualifications in the world but was quite a private individual and happy to follow along on Pyle's genius coat-tails. They got on very well; Robinson being the buffer between Pyle's eccentricity and the day to day work of the lab technicians, lined up at their workstations beyond a glass partition.

Also with the two scientists was Pyle's loyal Labrador, Naseby, sitting patiently until the cold tiles had him up and sniffing around – the room not yet needing to be sterile. Naseby went across to examine the 10 ft tall capsule which dominated the middle of the room, resembling a bob sled on its end, painted with the Union Jack colours, with all kinds of tubes and wires attached to it. Pyle and Robinson drifted after the dog and both looked in through the Perspex hood to the single seat with the heavy shoulder straps.

'We're good to go, I think,' said Pyle.

'I agree. Are you happy with the guinea pigs... sorry, the competition winners?'

'I'm delighted, old boy. They couldn't be better. The Mancunian wide-boy will go for it. The London lady has a boring life and loves her genealogy. She'll be keen. The American will no doubt be gung-ho.'

'Let Dr Mountfield go first, you think?'

'Yes, I think so. She'll come back from it whooping and high-fiving all and sundry.'

Robinson stroked Naseby on the head as he passed. 'I'm still not sure about this press woman being present. Our CCTV is covering everything. What if we have an unexpected problem?'

'Then we're finished, my dear fellow. I want a written record of these events whether we succeed entirely or whether we become infamous. Anyway, Robinson, stop with the negative vibes. Make final preparations while I plan our guests' welcome.'

***

Nathan had a brief walk to the garage to pick up his Audi A3. It had one of those matte grey paint jobs, courtesy of the previous owner. Nathan knew that particular finish looked ridiculous on some cars, but for his it seemed to work. The car was five years old, with a couple of dents where trees had jumped out at him, but still the best vehicle he had ever owned. He was dealt with by Gary, the garage owner, who had taken to cultivating huge sideburns in honour of his hero, TT motorbike legend, Guy Martin. As he listened to what work had been carried out, and then paid for it, Nathan could not take his eyes off the facial hair. He thanked Gary, and waved to the other mechanics as he left.

'Oi, Nathan!' shouted Gary, after him. 'By the way, your particulate filter light has come on.'

Nathan smiled wryly at him, then got in and drove away. The money he saved by way of a token road tax for having a clean engine, was spent up by having to take unnecessary trips up and down motorways to burn off the excess carbon. He took the Audi for a short spin around the airport and down the M56 motorway as far as Lymm village. Once the yellow light disappeared from the dashboard he headed for home.

***

Jada exited her apartment building in Chula Vista, hopped in her green VW Passat and drove to Pete's fire station. She had to sit and wait for a few minutes for his shift to end, before she could stand from the car and wave to him. He was extremely surprised to see her, as he said goodbye to his colleagues and jogged over to take her in his arms. He was immediately concerned that something was wrong.

'Oh, no, everything's great, baby,' she assured him. 'I just need to talk to you.'

'And it couldn't wait until I got home? Are you pregnant?'

'No, I'm not pregnant!' She laughed. 'Let's go to the beach.'

They took his vehicle, with him looking over to her at regular intervals, but she held her tongue until they reached La Jolla Shores, and parked up overlooking the Pacific ocean.

When they were settled, Jada gave Pete the envelope from Nigel Bissett. He read the contents slowly.

'Hey, girl, you've won!'

'I know! I never win anything. Except that garbage vampire book the other week.'

'You've won... what exactly have you won?'

'Well, it's an all expenses paid trip back to England. A thousand pounds spending money and a ten thousand pounds cheque on arrival. Then there'll be something special for me and the other two winners. So Nigel says.'

'Who's Nigel?'

'Nigel is the... man from England, who tells winners the good news.'

'And, when is this to happen?'

'Very soon.'

Pete transferred his gaze to the ocean. Then he referred back to the details on his lap. 'This Professor Pyle fella?'

'He's well known. He's a famous billionaire in Britain.'

Jada stared at Pete's profile. She trusted her boyfriend and deferred to his opinion on most things. But she was going back to England, whether he liked it or not.

'How did this come about?' he asked.

'Well, when I was in England with my sister tracing the family tree, we were flicking through a genealogy magazine. There was a competition in it.'

'What's his field, this professor? Medicine?'

'Genetics, I think. DNA.'

'Where will you be?'

'The Pyle estate in Surrey.'

He went quiet again for a moment.

'What, honey?' she asked.

'Are the other two winners women, as well?'

'I don't know.'

'I'm just thinking this Pyle man might be collecting, you know, concubines.'

Jada snorted with laughter. 'Concubines!? Where's that come from? Pete, I'm your concubine only.'

'That's good to hear. Hey, you're going to England, baby!'

***

Nathan was in his local pub, not with either girlfriend, just with some of the boys. The pub was called The Black Boar, although the picture had been blown away outside, revealing the pub's previous incarnation – a painting of the Duke of Wellington. Nathan was playing old school friend, Ollie, at darts. Ollie was a bit strange when it came to darts. He had his own game which he would play for hours. He would play out the entire World Snooker tournament in his head – if he scored more than sixty points in a visit to the oche, he won a frame. Anything under that and he lost the frame. Best of nineteen in the first round, building up to best of thirty-five in the final. People believed he imagined he was playing famous snooker players in his head. Apparently, he had been world snooker champion three times.

'Here's something we can do,' suggested Ollie. 'We both have six darts, and whatever the total is, that's the age we'll die at.'

Nathan drank some beer. 'Fucking hell, Ollie. What dark crevice did that one come from?'

'You go first.'

Shaking his head, Nathan took up position at the oche. He wondered whether he should play the percentages, stay away from the one and five alongside the twenty. He decided to have three at the treble twenty and three at other trebles. Off he went – twenty, treble five, treble five (worrying). Nineteen, three, seventeen. Total of eighty-nine. He was satisfied with that.

It was Ollie's turn – treble five, treble one, one (Nathan spluttering into his pint). Five, five, bounce out of the board. Three nearby friends screamed with laughter.

'Shit,' said Ollie, retrieving his dart from the floor. 'I've only got five more years to live.'

Nathan patted him on the back, gave his darts to someone else and moved towards the bar. It was then that he saw the Jehovah's Witness man, the man with the Maserati, in *his* pub, looking at *him*. Now it wasn't funny any more for Nathan. This was going to kick off big time. He looked about him for a weapon. He had his pint pot in his hand, but that didn't go down too well with magistrates at the moment. Better to pick up a wooden stool and bludgeon the man. As he approached, the man seemed to read his mind. He had that envelope out again and was making conciliatory gestures. When he could hear him above the pub music, Nathan could pick out, 'It's not what you think. It's... good. Trust...'

'What do you want, man?' Nathan challenged him.

'My name's Damon Julius...'

'I don't give a fuck what your name is. Why are you following me?'

'I have to deliver this letter. It's not unpleasant news, Mr Levy.'

'Mr Julius, if that *is* something I would prefer not to see, you're not going to be walking out of here. You may be able to look after yourself, but once I start on you, everyone in here starts on you.'

'I understand. Please, read it.'

Nathan took the envelope and opened it. He glanced at Damon before reading the contents. He was puzzled at first, then he relaxed and made an expression of resigned satisfaction.

'I think I remember entering this competition. Is this for real?' Damon nodded. 'Well, then. It's my round. What are you drinking? Have you been up to Manchester before? You'll find it's a very friendly place.'

FIVE

Carla sat with Warren Mansergh in the Broadway café in Bexleyheath. She had telephoned him with questions about the forthcoming event in Surrey, and was surprised that he seemed to be entirely at her disposal.

'Did you find a safe place to park the car?' she asked him.

'It's in a side street. Don't worry, if it gets stolen I'll just ring up for another one.'

Carla's eyes went wide at that comment – there was another example of the bizarre, enormous undertaking she was getting involved in. It was a world she wasn't even remotely connected to. Carla watched him. The well-dressed, successful young man seemed out of place in the little café, with the windows steamed up by the rain outside, but he was enjoying his toasted tea cake and his cup of coffee. He had even stood up to politely open the door for a harassed mother and her squalling toddler to go out.

'Was there something in particular you wanted to talk about, Carla?' he asked.

'No, no, all my questions seem to have merged into one feeling – fear. I'm frightened at what I'm getting involved with.'

'I wish I could ease your mind somewhat. I'm only told the logistics. The emotional side of going down there is all your own. I will say, on the few times I've met Professor Pyle, I've found him very upbeat and friendly. I shouldn't worry about staying down there.'

Carla sipped her tea.

'Are you married, Warren?'

'Married? No. I would have liked to be. But I blew my first

32

chance. I'm sure it will come along again in due course. On the subject of marriage, how did Mr Terry take the news?'

'He didn't take the news at all, because I haven't told him. I won't be telling him. He wouldn't understand. I'll just say I'll be going to stay with my mother for a while. Let the bugger fend for himself.'

Warren just nodded. He was pleased to have gotten this lovely lady as his assignment. He might have liked to go to California, but he was certainly happy not to have the Manchester man. He finished his coffee, and decided he wanted another – it was better than his filter variety at home. He stood up. 'More tea, Carla? On expenses.'

Carla smiled. 'Well, if it's on expenses, why not?'

He bought the fresh beverages and returned to their table.

'So, Carla, tell me. What got you interested in genealogy?'

'It has to be the BBC programme, *Who Do You Think You Are?* Before that started I knew absolutely nothing. I didn't even know who my grandparents were.'

'Really?'

'No, it was never something talked about in my house when I was growing up. What about you?'

'I've never looked into it.'

'Mansergh seems an Irish name to me.'

'Oh, there's nothing Irish about my family, I assure you.'

Carla gave him a look that said, "we'll see about that".

***

Damon Julius woke up in an armchair with absolutely no idea where he was. It was a small room, with a massive flat screen television. There were no photographs or ornaments on show – a very minimalist kind of place. Damon moved slightly and his head nearly exploded. *That'll be right*, he'd been drinking the night before. His phone was in his lap, but where was his jacket? Oh, there it was, covering some girl, asleep on the sofa. He had no idea who she was either.

He slowly managed to stand, and squinted through the window into a foggy Manchester morning. His Maserati sat there, unmolested. There were voices coming from, he presumed, the kitchen. Leaving his jacket where it was, as he could feel his wallet in his back pocket, Damon inched his way towards the sound. The smell of bacon frying hit him before he entered the kitchen, where he was faced with an extraordinary sight. The young woman, incidentally talking to cook, Nathan Levy, was wearing a bright red "onesie" sleep suit. It was shockingly figure-hugging, wonderful and bizarre at the same moment. On her feet were uncoordinated men's slippers. Her brown hair was piled up on top of her head in a sleepy mess and she wore glasses. She was smiling at him. Then he remembered she was the gorgeous Hannah he had been introduced to the previous night. There had been some snogging, he believed.

'Morning!' called Nathan, a little too enthusiastically. 'Bacon butty do you?'

'I'm sorry?' asked Damon.

'Hi,' said Hannah.

'Hi.'

'Sit down here. Nathan can do you a proper cooked breakfast. Did you sleep well there? Sorry, Naomi demanded the sofa.'

Damon sat down, devouring the contours of Hannah's body as he went.

'Bacon, eggs, sausages, then,' said Nathan. 'Sorry, no black pudding.'

Damon swallowed hard.

'Stop it, Nathan,' said Hannah, sitting next to Damon.

Damon focused on the pretty Hannah.

'Did you enjoy yourself last night?' asked Hannah. Damon just kept staring. 'You seemed a natural on the karaoke.'

'Karaoke?'

Then it started to come back to Damon – drinking heavily with

34

Nathan and his friends, and some idiot latecomer called Elvis, as well. A DJ setting himself up on the mini-stage in the corner. Girls arriving. Getting fairly drunk straightaway. Oh, God. Karaoke. He hated karaoke. What had he sung? He had a worrying feeling it had been something from Adele.

This Hannah had taken a shine to him, stopping him from becoming completely paralytic, fascinated that he was from London. They had "danced" late on. There had been kissing and some slight fumbling near the taxi, with avoidance of a fight between two men, then travelling the streets of south Manchester, managing to politely decline a kebab.

Another girl entered the kitchen to break up Damon's recollections. She also wore a ludicrously tight onesie outfit, this time in shocking pink. He immediately recognised her as Emma, Nathan's girlfriend. Or, at least, one of his girlfriends. That little revelation was remembered from the previous night.

Emma, though engrossed in the screen of her phone, kissed Nathan, smiled at Damon, then quickly made some tea and toast before departing again. Damon thought she must get by with the skills of a F1 driver racing through zero-visibility spray. He watched her bottom as it went by him. Hannah, leaning on the table between them, her face propped up on her two hands, looked on, still fascinated by the handsome southerner.

'I'll go and get dressed,' she said to Damon. 'Then we'll go back to mine. You can shower, and have more sleep if you need to. Then we'll do something with the day.'

She jumped up and skipped out of the kitchen before he could say a word either way.

Nathan laughed, placing a plate of food and cutlery down before Damon. 'She's got you now, mate.'

Damon shrugged as he looked at the greasy bacon and eggs. He tried to eat.

'Nathan?' asked Damon. 'Oh, thank you for putting me up, by the way. So, you've got two girlfriends, am I correct?' Nathan leant on a counter, drank his coffee and nodded. 'Do they know about each other?'

'I don't think so.'

'It's just, Emma's here. You said, Rachel was it? Rachel's just around the corner. What if she comes here?'

'Then she comes here.'

'Aren't you bothered, you know, by two worlds colliding?'

'Not really. If it happens, it happens.'

SIX

In San Diego, Nigel Bissett waited patiently for Jada's decision. Not that he was sitting around his hotel suite, because he had checked out of there and was currently staying with Jada's friend, Tracy. Since meeting in the restaurant, the two of them had been inseparable. They had made love the first night together – it was crazy, he knew, but he was already thinking about how to relocate to southern California. He found Tracy to be gorgeous, vivacious and possessing a lovely personality.

***

In London, Warren Mansergh had seen the area Carla lived in when he dropped her off at home. So he was quite happy in his luxury hotel suite. His situation was different to that of his colleagues because Carla was a sure thing – a genealogy nut who loved her dead relatives more than her living ones. He had tried to answer all her questions as best he could. Now it was just a case of waiting for the day to arrive when he would take her to the Pyle residence.

He was surprised when Carla rang him yet again. He was just out of the shower, thinking whether to contact his girlfriend to arrange a night out together.

Carla was twelve hours into researching Warren Mansergh's family tree. She had only paused to make her husband's sandwiches for work, and to do her morning lollipop lady shift near the school. Seeing the marriage and birth certificates and the census returns download had been just as much fun as if it had been her own family. She had the Mansergh family back to Warren's great, great grandfather, living in Hackney on the 1881 census, with a wife and five children. The man was down as being of Irish birth. Carla had also traced the family forward into the present day, and after a couple of frustrating brick walls had found a living relative of Warren's.

Warren Mansergh agreed to meet Carla at the library near her home. He was puzzled but happy to see her, and they embraced before she invited him to sit with her. It was then that he realised there was a smiling woman on the computer screen.

'I'm Skyping,' explained Carla. 'Warren, I'm connected to Dublin, and I want to introduce you to your cousin, Miss Catherine Mansergh.'

***

Damon Julius was also finding something of interest on the computer. Hannah was currently sexting him images of herself from her bedroom.

***

Jada came out of her apartment, allowing Nigel Bissett to take her luggage and place it in the boot of the Maserati. It was a cold, clear day in southern California. She had on jeans, an orange bubble jacket and her special travelling Adidas trainers, with her hair tied back into a pony-tail.

'Is Madam ready?' asked Nigel.

'Madam is. I'm so excited to be going back to England.'

Nigel got the passenger door for her.

'Do you think I'll be able to stay a while after going to the Pyle estate?'

'I don't see why not. Everyone else can stay. If you ask nicely the government will give you a mansion in Mayfair and a grand a month in benefits.'

As they drove towards the airport, Jada watched the streets pensively.

'So,' said Nigel, 'you're looking forward to seeing England again?'

'Very much so. Tell me, Nigel, will Surrey be very different to Wolverhampton?'

Nigel just laughed uproariously.

***

In London, Carla was given a gentlemanly hand into the Maserati by Warren Mansergh. The weather was grim and overcast, the streets still wet from a recent shower.

'Have you got everything you need, Mrs Terry?'

'I think so, Warren. It won't take us long, will it?'

'Not long at all.'

'Will I see you during my stay?'

'I'm afraid not, no. I'll bring you home, though. Hopefully you'll have an exciting time to tell your husband about.'

Carla said nothing to that. She watched Warren jog around to the driver's side and then checked for nosy neighbours as they drove away.

***

'Surrey? Okay, babe. Send me a text when you get there.'

Nathan placed down a cup of tea on the cabinet alongside Emma in her bed. He kissed her on the left temple, without disturbing her intense focus on her iPhone, and left her house.

'Surrey!? What the fuck is going on in Surrey!? I swear, Nathan, if you're not in my car for Sheffield tomorrow morning, then we're through.'

Nathan, carrying a black holdall, came out of his house to a waiting Damon Julius. Damon took the luggage from him.

'Lovely day for it,' said Nathan, thinking the Londoner had expected it to rain constantly in Manchester.

'It certainly is, sir.'

'Do me a favour, will you. Don't call me sir.'

'Sure.'

'Any chance I can do the driving?'

'Feel free. It's not my car.'

Nathan got into the driver's seat, waited for Damon to get in alongside him, then drove away at speed.

'How did the girlfriends take the news?' asked Damon.

Nathan laughed involuntarily. 'You could say a mixed response. Towards the motorways, is it?'

'Yes.'

They turned right at the main road and sped up to the next junction. All along they passed a mass of road works and chopped-down trees.

'They're building an extension to the tram system,' Nathan pointed out. 'Six years it's going to take them – the lazy bastards. In China or Japan it would take seven months.'

Nathan turned right onto Ringway road just as a plane came in low to land at Manchester airport. Nathan settled in, positioned his hands on the wheel where professional racing drivers put them and gunned the Maserati.

'Next left,' said Damon.

Nathan slowed, amused at the shortest ever joy ride.

'We're not driving down to Surrey, then?'

'Sorry, no. We're going by helicopter.'

'Fair enough.'

Nearing take-off, Nathan and Damon were in the back of the

40

helicopter behind two pilots. Everyone wore headphones and were able to communicate. Nathan turned to Damon. 'You know, I've lived here all my life and never flown out of Manchester airport.'

'You have flown, though? You're not going to freak out?'

'Oh, yeah, I'm fine.'

'Here we go.' He indicated the pilots. 'These two guys here work for the company? So they're under your instruction.'

'Yes, they are.'

Nathan enjoyed the novelty of being airborne inside the perimeter of the airport, then leant forward to the pilots. 'Gentlemen, we need to head out in that direction.'

'Mr Julius?' checked the head pilot.

'Yes, go with that,' answered Damon. 'If we're allowed to.'

A minute later the helicopter was over Nathan's district.

'This is right,' said Nathan. 'Right, good, that block of flats. Go really low over those.' Nathan sat back laughing, delighted. 'Buzz those flats! Buzz them! Okay, drift over to the left a bit. To port. A bit more. Hover just here, mate. Great!'

Nathan leant across Damon and they looked down to where a woman was pruning roses in her garden.

'Everyone, wave to my mother!'

'Won't the helicopter disturb her?' asked Damon.

'No, no. She's had the police helicopter above her house enough times with me over the years.'

Nathan and Damon enjoyed a good laugh.

SEVEN

Jason Kanini had once thought Shrewsbury in Shropshire a wonderful place to live, although only having St Helens on Merseyside and Winsford in Cheshire to compare it to had made it an easy conclusion. The town had everything a single twenty-two-year-old man could want – plenty of single women, pubs and restaurants, as well as enough heritage and beautiful architecture, which also floated his boat. After sitting on the sunny banks of the river Severn one summer's afternoon, he had even talked to the people who ran one of the rowing clubs about the possibility of him joining.

Jason was one of those people who seemed to have done every job in the book: bartender, cook, condom vending machine filler, charity mugger, bus driver for disabled children. Shrewsbury had begun brightly enough with a position in his friend's roof-cleaning business (leaving maroon roofs sticking out like sore thumbs on roads of houses with grey tiles), until that friend had decided to drop everything and go back-packing around Thailand for a year. A security guard job had followed, and then his current position as a sort of concierge/doorman for a pretentious company of architects in the Castle Foregate district. It was an open plan building, which they probably designed themselves, where everything from the front desk to the architects at work in the rear could be seen from the street. That put Jason off straightaway, not having anywhere to even grab a moment's peace while on duty, but his fellow reception staff were really nice and, besides, there was always Adelaide Pyle to look at.

Adelaide Pyle, Professor Pyle's twenty-four-year-old daughter from his first marriage, was a senior partner in the business, coerced up from London to Shrewsbury by an old university pal. Adelaide was blonde, almost beautiful enough to ask people not to hate her for it. She was attractive in a rich, horsey-set kind of way, too much expensive dental work and designer gear, the sort of person who never had to worry about paying bills, because her bills were re-routed elsewhere before she even saw them.

For all that, she had a cute side, a playful side, was only 5ft 6ins, with tiny feet and hands with the nails chewed to buggery, and just the most glorious, tight little bottom. At least, that was Jason Kanini's opinion of it on the few times he had managed to see it in the buff.

All her colleagues were boorish, coke-snorting pricks – again, Jason's opinion. He of no education, university or otherwise, born to a single mum in a council flat, but with more common-sense, intelligence and trustworthiness than the lot of them put together. They all shunned him, either there on the premises, or if they crossed paths out and about in Shrewsbury town centre. They seemed to have confused feelings about the fact that Adelaide had a soft spot for him; some of the women half understood it, some plainly found it unbelievable for her to mess about with the concierge; a few of the men were apathetic towards it, a couple clearly had a huge problem with him. Perhaps it was jealousy on their part.

Adelaide was Jason's most complicated relationship so far. Of course, in later years, he would be able to understand her moody, confused female behaviour, but at twenty-four it was all encompassing for his emotions to handle. She blew hot and cold – wanting him, finding him attractive, then changing her mind and backing him off, only allowing a casual relationship that existed just above friendship. Their physical relationship was less than he was used to, making love just the handful of times. Other intimacies performed by him were received almost guiltily, as if there was a religious or class barrier she was trying to get beyond – and the compliment was strangely never reciprocated. If he had told his friends that last fact, they would have laughed their heads off and told him to kick her selfish butt into the long grass.

Despite these difficulties, Jason and Adelaide generally enjoyed each other's company. There was just something about her; she was what he wanted more than anything at that time in his life.

One of the male architects who had the problem with Jason, approached the front desk, showing an oddly cheesy smile to the seated receptionist, and barely nodding to Jason, who stood there in his plain black suit and thirty pound shoes. Jason wanted to move away from the man, but as it was his job to be there, he was a bit stuck. The man's name was Tom Knott, a smarmy, arrogant son-of-a-bitch if ever there was one. He was taller than Jason, wearing a brighter-than-bright white shirt with serious red braces. He was waiting to greet a client. He talked to the receptionist, while completely ignoring Jason. The first chance she got, the receptionist shot a glance at Jason that said she thought Knott was a complete arsehole as well.

***

Lynette Pyle, Professor Pyle's first wife and mother of Adelaide, was not at her home in Jamaica, which had been part of her divorce settlement. Instead, she was at her flat in Kensington, London, standing in her kitchen, preparing lunch for the visit of her sister. It was taking her a while because she was staring out of the window at people passing by and at builders with their overloaded skip across the road, but not really seeing anything, as her mind ticked over furiously. She had just returned from Selfridges, where surprisingly she had bumped into a woman by the name of Jane Royle; Jane being Professor Pyle's personal assistant of over ten years standing. With Pyle having just been nominated by the Nobel Prize committee, it was inconceivable that Jane would not be at his side, yet there she was with a friend, shopping without a care in the world. Lynette had hailed the woman warmly, before launching into what amounted to an interrogation, which proved wholly unsatisfactory. Apparently, Jane was on paid gardening leave, unclear as to why she had been sent away from the Surrey mansion. She had assured Lynette that Pyle was in good health, that there had been no fall-out, that there had been whispers about a strange genealogy magazine competition, then she had made her excuses to move off with her impatient friend.

Genealogy magazine competition, mused Lynette. It was just plain bizarre. The man had never shown any interest in it before. She knew he had been adopted as a baby in the Fifties. She threw down the knife she was using; she was determined to find out what the old fool was up to, so went to her phone book to ring Adelaide, her other children and any and all possible relations.

***

On the evenings that Adelaide allocated to Jason, they usually used his rented flat in the town centre as a base. She owned a 17th century cottage north of the town, at Battlefield, with a view of the magnificent St Mary Magdalene church. Unlike her, Jason loved it there and appreciated its heritage value, but he had only been invited twice.

Actually, he didn't care where they were, as long as he could be near to Adelaide. As he watched her doing her make-up in his bathroom one Friday night, topless except for a cream bra, he brought up the subject of his brother's twenty-first birthday party in Winsford. She had looked at him slowly along her mascara wand.

'Winsford, Jason, really?'

'Well, I can drive you in with a blanket over you, and do the same on the way out, if you don't want to be seen there.'

She continued with what she was doing in silence.

'My family want to meet you,' he added.

'Why on earth would they want to do that?'

'Because... isn't that what normal people do?'

'Are you saying I'm not normal?'

'No, that just came out wrong. Listen, you don't have to think about Winsford.'

'There's nothing to stop you going, of course.'

'That's good of you,' he replied, sarcastically.

'Jason, we're not going to have one of those nights, are we?'

He shook his head at her. She leant out of the bathroom for a kiss.

They had a very pleasant evening out together in Shrewsbury – she was lovely to him; they chatted to mutual acquaintances, laughed, drank quite a bit of wine. They settled into a relaxed mood together – Jason wondering why it couldn't always be that way; and, in fact, she had closed down again by the time they were walking back to his flat, with a bag of chips shared between them.

Something sparked the subject of family once more. He joked about one day being invited to meet her parents.

'There you go again!' she snapped. 'It's not as if you're a serious boyfriend, or anything.'

He stopped dead; other revellers had to swerve around them. 'Why do you say that? I know I'm serious about this. I just don't get you at all.' Her expression told him that she was not willing to discuss it. He threw the remnants of the chips into a plastic bin. 'Adelaide, we're so good together. We are, aren't we? Admit it.'

'All right, I admit it. I do want you, Jason. Just not in the way you want.'

'I know I don't pressure you. God, I put up with so much crap from you. Just spell it out to me. What is your problem?'

By some miracle of logistics, two police officers happened to be passing along the pedestrianised road. Adelaide used their presence as a way of ending the discussion, 'Jason, you're making a scene. I'm going home alone.'

'Adelaide!'

'Let's leave it for now, Jason.'

'Adelaide!'

She skipped away into groups of passers-by. Infuriated beyond belief by her once more, Jason punched the plastic bin, causing a huge dent. The policemen looked over their shoulders briefly, but then continued on.

It was a couple of days before Jason saw Adelaide again. He was on duty at the architects' – saw her coming along the road through the glass frontage. She had on a small leather jacket and a loud, red tartan mini-skirt over black leggings. Normally he would have kidded her about the skirt, but he was content to just stand there and say hello. She came through the rotating door and completely blanked him as if he wasn't there, even as his words of welcome died on his lips. Jason was astonished. He watched her skip over to her colleagues without a care in the world, especially to the cheesy Tom Knott with his awful, false grin. Jason would have gone after her across the ground floor, but clients were piling in on him. He decided to remain professional (if that term applied to his position), keep working, let her come to him.

But she blanked him again as she went to lunch. Jason just watched her go by, without attempting to speak to her. His stomach dropped to the floor with the silly sadness of it all – silly, because she was acting like a child, and taking him there with her.

Jason's lunch break coincided with Adelaide's return, so he missed her passing him in reception again. He had to stand there all afternoon watching her work, seeing her hair swish about, and that ridiculous skirt move between desks and between people. As she left for the night, he attempted to speak with her again, only to be rebuffed in a similarly horrible fashion. She happened to be leaving with Tom Knott – Jason only had eyes for Adelaide, but he sensed Knott's hostility towards him.

The following day, while many young people would have walked away from the situation, he turned up for work. He chatted with his reception colleagues and ran the usual errands for the architects. Adelaide was a no-show. A discreet enquiry told him she was meeting a client out on-site somewhere.

Tom Knott approached him, out of the blue, mid-afternoon.

'Adelaide's with me now,' he said to Jason.

Jason struggled to comprehend the words. *With you*, you ugly ignoramus? Adelaide wasn't with anyone – she didn't know how to be with anyone. What did the man mean? It was illogical.

'You'll have to stop trying to talk to her,' continued Knott.

Thinking it through later in his flat, Jason realised he had not responded to Knott's words. The man had just gone away from him. The rest of the shift had gone by in a daze.

The rest of the week had just been, frankly, blackly ridiculous. Jason, in full masochistic fashion, stood by that door and watched such a cruel display of female affection poured out towards Knott – coquettish touches, giggles for no reason, holding of hands on the way to lunch. Everything that had proved tricky between herself and Jason was now openly there on show with the new "couple".

Jason thought he was going slowly mad, doubting his own reading of the situation – after all, he didn't have a God-given right to be with her. Obviously she saw something he didn't in Knott. But two receptionists commented on the absurdity of the pairing – "He's such a total creep" was one comment, and even two architects were overheard at the water cooler voicing similar opinions.

Still Jason didn't quit. He faced up to the cruelty in which Adelaide Pyle inflicted on him day after day, still knowing that he wanted her and that he was the better man. He convinced himself that she didn't know what she was doing. That she had fallen in with Knott because she was emotionally confused. But how long would it take her to see that?

Work kept Adelaide away sporadically, and then, Jason overheard, some family emergency in Surrey saw her disappear from Shrewsbury altogether.

EIGHT

At Pyle's mansion, Carla wanted to pull the antique doorbell chain, but the huge oak door swung open as she approached across the white gravel drive and a butler politely gestured for her to enter. Oh, he's fantastic, she thought. If only he could have said, *you rang?* She stepped over the threshold very tentatively.

'Welcome to the Pyle residence, Mrs Terry,' said Pringle, groomed and very upright. 'My name's Pringle. I'll be looking after your needs.'

'Thank you, Pringle.'

The noise of a helicopter passed over them before he shut the door.

'Sounds like our final guest is arriving. Would you follow me, please?'

And he walks slowly, thought Carla, grinning. Fabulous. Pringle opened a door for her and she walked into what was the Drawing Room. Jada stood from a sofa to offer her a loud American welcome.

'Well, hi there. I guess we're two of the lucky winners. I'm Jada.'

They shook hands.

'I'm Carla, hello. Are you American?'

'Certainly am. I live in San Diego, California. You?'

'Bexleyheath. London.'

'Come and sit. We've champagne.'

'Champagne? Goodness, I've not had champagne for over ten years.'

Jada poured the bubbly.

'Are you hungry?' asked Jada. 'I've got Pringle running back and forth to the kitchen.'

'No, I'm too excited to eat.'

They both clinked glasses and laughed. After sipping the champagne, Carla looked round the room, then stretched to take in a view over the grounds.

'What a place,' she said to Jada.

'You're not wrong.'

'Have you been here long?'

'About an hour. I presume I'm from the furthest away so they brought me first. Very secretive, though. They won't answer any of my questions.'

'I've not asked any. No, I think if I make a noise they might discover they've got the wrong person and take me straight home again.'

'No, girl, you're a winner. I can tell.'

'So, this is to do with the genealogy magazine? I love family history, do you?'

'I've enjoyed doing it, certainly. Some of my family come from England originally. I believe it's called the Black Country, around Wolverhampton.'

'Oh, yes.'

'And then it's all Alabama. Lawyers and doctors.'

'Wonderful. I'm all East End of London. Costermongers, dock workers, prostitutes.'

Nathan stepped from the helicopter and laughed at the golf buggy and its po-faced driver, waiting to take him to the big house. He turned back and did the upside-down tennis handshake with his new friend, Damon Julius. 'You're a star, Damon. You've told me absolutely nothing, you're a pro at what you do.'

'Enjoy yourself, Nathan. I'll go back and look after your Rachel for you.'

'You do that, mate.'

Nathan did the unnecessary bend to avoid decapitation by the rotor blades, jogged over to the buggy and let himself be taken over the grass. On the ride in, he looked at the roller-coaster to his left and the ski slope to his right. 'Fucking hell.'

He was greeted by Pringle and taken in to meet Jada and Carla. Jada was on champagne duty again.

'Sound,' said Nathan, thanking her by using Mancunian slang for the first time in a decade. Maybe he was nervous, he concluded, as he took the offered champagne flute. He looked about him at the dark panelled walls and the deep alcove windows.

'Have you come far?' asked Carla.

'Manchester.'

'I'm from London. Jada's the international around here. San Diego.'

'Oh, shit, San Diego,' said Nathan to Jada, 'I'm a Denver Broncos fan, sorry.'

'I won't hold it against you,' she replied.

'Are we it, then?' Nathan asked. 'What's the plan?'

'We'll meet Professor Pyle soon,' said Carla. 'Hopefully he'll explain exactly what we've won.'

'Ten grand, isn't it? Maybe some spending money, as well. Do you want something more?'

'I'm hoping he'll give me my own professional researcher to get further on my family tree. Something like that.'

Jada touched her arm. 'Oh, Carla, that would be wonderful.'

Nathan said, 'I just want to go on the man's roller-coaster.'

'How about the ski-jump?' asked a new, female voice behind him.

Lucy and Jackson entered the room. Nathan blatantly looked Lucy up and down. He saw that type of lovely blonde woman who no doubt had been jaw-dropping as a teenager, now sexy in a sophisticated way with shorter, sensible hair and that "just off glowing" complexion.

'I'll pass on that, thank you,' he told her.

For a moment Lucy checked out Nathan as well. She found a

52

handsome, unshaven, cocky northerner.

'May I introduce us?' she asked of the group. 'I'm Lucy, this is Jackson. We're the exclusive Press for this event. Jackson will be taking photographs non-stop. He hasn't much conversation so don't bother talking to him.'

On cue, Jackson took all their photographs.

Carla asked, 'Could you give us some idea of the itin... the time thing of our stay?'

'Well, I think Professor Pyle is going to ask you to take part in an experiment. I know that sounds ominous, but I'm sure it's not. If you don't like what he has to say you can take your cheque and go.'

'I won't unpack, then,' said Nathan.

Pyle came into the room, very jolly, and went around shaking everyone's hand, introducing himself. 'Have you all got some champagne? Good. Jolly good. Your rooms are ready for you. My house is your house, as long as you're not still here at Christmas.' He stood looking at them all. 'I know you're all puzzled, so I won't drag things out further.'

Pyle glanced to see that Lucy was taking shorthand notes.

'I can't wait, professor,' she told him, deadpan.

'Genealogy!' continued Pyle, 'What a fabulous thing, unearthing lost information and images from your family's past. You love it, don't you, Carla? May I call you Carla? If an ancestor had made just the slightest of different decision, he would never had met that woman, never have had your grandfather. And then all the thousands of twists of fate that produces who we are. What if you could step back in time for a few minutes? Look at an ancestor's life. Be a ghost at their shoulder. They don't know you're there while you savour seeing what they're doing at that particular time, but more importantly what...they... look like. What they look like! Great-grandmother Mary in 1875, great-great-grandfather William at the Battle of Waterloo, your grandfather when he was a boy. Jada, what do you think?'

'It sounds fabulous, professor.'

'Nathan, what about you?'

'Sounds like a science fiction novel. Can I ask a question? When do we get to...' He glanced at Lucy. 'eat. I'm starving.'

'Immediately after this meeting,' Pyle told him, with a little smile on his lips for the wide-boy. 'What did you say, a science fiction novel? That's good. But what if it could really happen? What if, in your DNA, sat everything that ever happened to your ancestors? It's in you, it just needs to be shaken up and brought to the fore.'

Pyle walked about the room, smiling for Jackson's lens, pleased with how things had started with his three guests. Then he continued.

'Let me tell you a story. When I was sixteen I chased after a girl called Emma Albright-Hussey. Not sure why, because she was rather plain, flat-chested and always wore those leggings with the straps that go under the feet. Terrible fashion item. But I persisted, and got her. It was a very boring relationship. I pretended I liked the unusual name, that it was a bit risqué. Twenty years later, because I love genealogy, as you all do, and was tracing family relatives, I discovered that in the 18th century an ancestor on my mother's side called June Pugh actually lived in a building called Albright-Hussey in Shropshire. It's still there as a luxury hotel, overlooking the place where the Battle of Shrewsbury happened in 1403, but I digress. What I'm trying to say, is that place name came down through the generations of my family without me hearing it out loud and sat in my subconscious, so much so that I just had to date that awful girl.'

'Professor,' said Jada, 'could it just be deja-vu? Coincidence?'

'Well, perhaps, Jada, but she wasn't called Emma Bristol.'

'When I was seventeen,' interjected Nathan, 'I'd just passed my driving test and was allowed to drive my parents on holiday to North Wales. My dad always took the coast road, but I went inland, and had the strangest feeling that I'd been to that part of Wales before. It was impossible, though.'

'There you go,' said Pyle, with a big smile. 'Anyway, that's enough of that for now. Please, if you would, go through that way and my staff are waiting to serve some refreshments.'

Nathan led the way to the dining room, next door. Liveried waiters stood ready to serve. Nathan sat down and moved the next chair out for Lucy. She took it.

'You'd better interview me first,' he told her. 'I might be gone after this meal.'

'Do you promise to be interesting?'

'I'll try my best.' He turned to a waiter. 'Can I have a steak, mate? Medium. With fries or potatoes, or whatever.'

The waiter accepted his order, as well as getting him and Lucy drinks. With his stomach on a promise, Nathan gave his full attention to Lucy.

'So, why are you here?' she asked him.

'My mother entered me. She likes little competitions.'

'So, you're not as crazy about genealogy as you're supposed to be?'

'Not really. I did some family research for my mum but it's all passed me by. When I'm older I might be interested.'

'What did you find in your research?'

'I found thirty-two agricultural labourers, a lot of people moving around the country, and a bit of incest in Lincolnshire.'

'Did no-one's life catch your attention?'

'A couple of men lived to be ninety and had three wives. My great-grandfather was in the Royal Navy and crashed his first ship into the Bell Rock lighthouse.'

Lucy giggled. 'He's just got to be interesting.'

Their drinks arrived. They clinked glasses.

Across the table, Jada and Carla sat together deep in conversation.

'Oh, it is addictive, genealogy,' Carla was saying, 'Just wanting to get that next clue that shows where a missing ancestor is.'

'I agree. A couple of times I was stumped, but then another way presented itself. What do you think the professor intends for us?'

'I'm puzzled. What was all that about seeing what our ancestors looked like? Perhaps he's got some rare old photographs.'

'I hope so.'

Nathan indicated Jackson to Lucy. 'I would have thought the professor would have insisted on a film crew, not a still photographer.'

'There are cameras everywhere recording it all. The professor wanted me to cover this story, and Jackson's with me.'

'Jackson's with you?'

'Yes. Jackson and I are recently divorced.'

'Really? That's interesting.'

'Yes, isn't it?'

NINE

Pyle and his assistant, Dr Robinson, led their house guests into the laboratory, where they all fanned out around the capsule. Jackson madly took photographs, having to step over the connecting lines as he did so. Lucy, with the most concerned expression of them all, stood alongside Nathan.

'I nominate Carla,' joked Nathan.

'I second that,' said Jada.

'What *is* this?' asked Carla.

Pyle coughed to clear his throat. 'Ladies and gentlemen. Here's the genie in the bottle. Genie-alogy.' He laughed. 'The machine that will give you all three wishes. Nathan, yes, I see you want to comment.'

'I'll take £10m, a box at the Etihad stadium and Frankie out of the *Saturdays*.'

'Ah, you must remember it has to do with genealogy. Think of three wishes to do with the people on your family tree.'

Nathan's face remained blank.

'You, Carla,' prompted Pyle. 'What are your three wishes to do with your family?'

'I've got three things that come to mind,' she answered, 'but I don't really understand what you're getting at.'

Pyle raised his hands. 'Yes, I'm sorry. Time for me to stop faffing about and put you out of your misery. Dr Robinson here will be happy to explain the mechanics of what I'm going to say, but I'll get straight to the point. We can take you to have a glimpse, for about ten minutes, at any ancestor you choose, somewhere within the lifetime you tell us, anywhere in the past.'

The silence in the room was beyond stunned. Carla had a touch of tinnitus, in her left ear mostly, and it seemed very loud there and then.

Jada finally spoke up for them all. 'Are you saying, Professor, that this... is a time machine?'

'Yes, I suppose I am,' answered Pyle. 'Not the kind you see in the movies. We can't send you back and put you on the grassy knoll in Dallas. Well, not unless an ancestor was actually there, and even then it would be pot luck during their lifetime. We, how shall we say, shake up your DNA, find the connection to the time your ancestor lived, and put you back there.'

Jada asked another question, 'Professor, has this been tried before?'

'Yes, Dr Mountfield, it has.'

Nathan leant towards Lucy and whispered, 'Doctor? I thought she was a model.'

'How exactly?' asked Jada.

'A number of animals, fitted with tiny video cameras. When they returned we could see... well, other animals around them on screen.'

Nathan laughed.

'I think we get it, mate,' he said. 'I'm not sure if I believe it, though.'

Carla touched Nathan's arm. 'May I suggest we go to our rooms and give this some thought?'

'Do what you want, love. I'm going for a kip, then I'll collect my cheque, thank you very much, and I'm out of here.'

He then edged away from the crazy discussion. Lucy, recording the conversation, exchanged looks with him.

'I would have thought a man from Manchester,' she said to him, 'would be "mad for it".'

Nathan grinned. 'Are you willing to go?'

Dr Robinson gently accosted Nathan. 'Perhaps a quiet chat would help you understand the procedure?'

'I'm quite happy not understanding it. I might listen to you explain how I would survive it.'

Pyle clapped his hands together.

'Carla's right,' he said. 'Please, retire to your rooms. Just mull over what you've come across here. When you come down we can talk in more detail. Think about all the hours spent on your family tree searching all those names, and imagine if you could see them as clearly as you see each other in this room.'

Nathan led them all out of the laboratory.

Carla wandered barefoot about her luxury bedroom, with its four-poster double bed and the type of modern art on the walls that her husband would not have bothered saving from one of his skips. She checked her view for the fifth time – yes, the woods were still there.

'Good grief. Good heavens.'

She sat down on the bed and twiddled her top lip. Deep down, she believed she knew what she would decide to do. A hobby she adored and long-since dead names that she loved, against years of domestic drudgery and numbing boredom. It was just a matter of finding a way to get herself to that decision. And being brave enough.

Jada, in her room, failed to get a signal on her mobile and threw it on the bed. She needed advice; she needed help, she needed fireman Pete at home in San Diego. She felt a little nauseous. Deep breaths, girl. Deep breaths. For probably the most intelligent guest there, she found she could not even begin to concentrate on what she had just heard – her mind was cotton candy. She realised that her body was sweating unnaturally with unused adrenalin, so went through to start the shower running in the bathroom. When it was a safe temperature she stripped and put herself under the jet. That helped, she thought. The water took some of the stress away. Genealogy; she started thinking of the great times when she discovered who someone's parents were, where they came from, wondering what brought them from *there* of all places. The photo's she'd found, lovely sepia ones of serious old-timers outside courthouses in the twenties, of loved ones she'd known as a very little girl when they were her age now, working at a gas station in somewhere like Columbiana, Alabama. She started to cry, in a good way, and sank down the wall to sit in the shower base. It made her feel better. She felt proud of her people; she was there because of them all, and she would not let them down.

In his room, with a teasing view of the roller-coaster, Nathan had found the mini-bar.

Lucy and Jackson took a long walk, over the perfectly mowed lawns and off into the extensive grounds. They looked at each other a few times to see if there was any comprehension at all of what had just happened. They came across the tennis courts and found the first hole of a pitch and putt golf course. Up a steep rise through the conifer trees they put arms around each other's waists to steady themselves, not thinking for a second whether divorced people did that kind of thing. They expected to see the boundary of Pyle's land, perhaps a church steeple or a public road. Instead, they found a full-size race track laid out below them. It staggered them both.

'Bloody hell,' said Jackson. 'This guy's not messing about.'

***

'Thank you, Pringle,' said Pyle, for the tray of tea placed on his desk. He waited for his butler to silently depart before looking at Dr Robinson.

'Shall I be mother?' asked Robinson, reaching to pour. 'How do you think that went?'

'As well as could be expected.'

'I wonder what three things they'll focus on.'

'Robinson, you're assuming they're still in the building. But if they are, their choices can be no weirder than yours.'

'Ah, but I've no intention of going through with them. Unlike your good self.'

'True,' said Pyle, accepting a cup. 'I'll be visiting the ancestors who interest me the most.'

'But not before your guinea pigs?'

***

Nathan, carelessly carrying a glass of whisky from his room, found Lucy, Carla and Jada via the Drawing room, the Snooker room and the Library. They were sitting in a small, modern lounge area, lit through French windows from an inner courtyard, with wide-screen television, games consoles and music systems, all drinking tea or coffee and with their feet up beneath them on leather sofas.

'Is Colonel Mustard anywhere to be found?' he asked them.

Only Carla understood that he was alluding to the *Cluedo* board game, but none of the women were very interested in his comment.

'Have you had a nice rest?' asked Lucy.

'It's been great, thanks. What are we discussing, genealogy?'

'What else is there to talk about after all that?' asked Jada.

Nathan seated himself. For all the age of Pyle's mansion, he found the place to be very comfortable and welcoming.

'How are you feeling?' he asked Jada.

'Honestly? Terrified. But also genuinely excited. I feel like I've been asked to go on a vital space mission.'

Nathan laughed, then sought Carla's opinion.

'Well,' Carla said, 'in the words of Richard Gere in *An Officer and a Gentleman*, I've got nowhere else to go. My life went from normal to downright boring a long time ago. As with Jada, I'm excited about this. You?'

'Me? I'm taking my ten grand and getting out.'

Under her breath, Lucy said, 'Coward.'

Nathan laughed again. 'Would you go, Lucy?'

'Not a cat in hell's chance,' she replied. 'Nathan, tell me, please, what are you afraid of?'

'What am I afraid of? Lucy, babe, when I had my tonsils out I was a nervous wreck. I was convinced I wasn't going to wake up. Now this clown wants to split me into atoms and fire me back into the past. No, thank you.'

'Don't you want to look at your grandfather when he was a boy? Or see your great-grandmother getting married? Or… what else? Maybe you'll find yourself alongside a relative at the Battle of Waterloo.'

'As a cannonball takes his fucking head off. Sorry, I didn't mean to swear. Listen, don't get me wrong, I love the idea. I just don't like the method of getting there.'

'How did you get here?' asked Lucy.

'What?'

'You came by helicopter, right? I see about four helicopter crashes a year on the news. If that had gone down between Manchester and here, it would have turned you to atoms.'

'The lady makes a good point,' said Jada. 'Life's fragile. We could go at any moment. I don't smoke or do bungee jumps. Maybe that's why I'm taking the risk with Professor Pyle.'

Nathan looked at each of the women in turn.

'You think I should live dangerously?' he asked.

'Only you can decide,' said Carla. 'It's a case of weighing your journey against what you might find on the other side.'

Everyone laughed at that.

'On the other side,' said Nathan. 'An unfortunate turn of phrase there, Carla.'

***

62

For the rest of the day it was as if nothing extraordinary had been said. Nathan played snooker with Jackson. The room had mahogany panelling on the walls, red leather smoking chairs and an antique set of green light shades over the table, the kind Nathan had seen once when a Premiership footballer had let the cameras into his mansion for a "cribs" show.

When conversation proved hard to come by with Jackson, including snippets of information concerning Lucy, Nathan took the game very seriously and ended up winning by eight frames to one. At least Jackson proved to be a no quitter. Pringle never faltered in his delivery of snacks and alcoholic beverages. Both men were slightly drunk, come the evening.

Jada and Carla took their turn for a long walk through the grounds, taking Naseby the Labrador along with them. On returning, tired and thirsty, they met Angela the cook and she invited them into the kitchen and provided them with tea and sandwiches, as well as telling them some of the history of the house long before the eccentric professor bought it. Jada and Carla were fascinated to hear about three generations of Angela's family being in service there, back to just after the Great War.

Lucy had turned her phone off and driven away in her Audi A1 in search of a village to do some shopping and to look at some regular members of the public who hadn't heard what she had heard that day. Unable to make a decision on where to stop, she found herself continuing on until she hit the town of Godalming. There she bought toiletries and sweets and some of those glazed doughnuts that Jackson liked so much. She had tea and a scone in a quaint little tea shop, walked around for another two hours, then went into a pizza place for a starter nibble and a glass of red wine, just waiting for it to go dark outside.

Seeing as everyone seemed to need peace and solitude, Pyle also decided to take a break from proceedings. He put on his biker leathers and helmet and walked over to his industrial-sized garage, from where he took his beloved Harley Davidson out onto the twisting Surrey B roads. It was a joyous hobby of his, motorcycling, one he had come to late in life. Britain and France had hosted his travels so far, but he wondered if he was getting too old to do the American journey. Eventually, he forced himself to head back and arrived just ahead of Lucy's Audi.

The evening meal at the Pyle residence had just the three guests at the table. Nothing much was said and the two women went to bed early – Jada announcing she was feeling the effects of the flight from California. Nathan found that television lounge area again and watched Spanish football and *The Walking Dead* zombie series before turning in himself.

By breakfast the next morning, it seemed, they had all had a good think. As he strolled in, Nathan found Lucy and Jackson drinking coffee over by the windows. Jada and Carla were clearly discussing their three most important ancestors.

Nathan was hungover. There was a shy waitress lingering, to whom he whispered that he would like "egg in bread" with brown sauce. She was none the wiser. Nathan turned to Carla who was discussing the English Civil War with an enthralled Jada.

'Carla, what's the proper name for egg in bread?'

'French toast.'

'Thank you.'

The waitress was okay with that and went away. Nathan poured himself black coffee and bid good morning to the two journalists.

'So, you're good at snooker, I hear,' said Lucy.

'That's Manchester schools for you.'

'Pyle's good as well, apparently.'

'I'll have to play him with my ten grand.' He took a seat and sat on it back to front. 'I take it my fellow winners have made up their minds. Probably best not to think too technically about it. If you're going to do it, just jump straight in, that's what I think.'

'What about you?' Lucy asked.

'Let me have my French toast first.'

After breakfast, Pringle made an appearance to invite them all into Pyle's office. Nathan brought up the rear, doing his best Liam Gallagher walk, and took the last luxuriant armchair, looking up at Professor Pyle and Dr Robinson, with their expectant faces.

'Professor Pyle,' spoke up Carla, 'I've been elected to speak for everyone.'

'Please, Carla, go ahead.'

'Myself and Jada, Jada and I, are willing to participate in this, but only after discussing every detail with Dr Robinson.'

Nathan pulled an expression to suggest he now thought his fellow winners were not such lemmings after all.

'And Nathan?' asked Pyle.

'Oh, Nathan's in,' said Carla. 'But instead of speaking to Dr Robinson, he'd just like to go on your roller-coaster.'

Pyle laughed heartily, delighted, looked at a smiling Robinson who was hiding his relief.

'Jolly good show!' said Pyle. 'That's excellent!'

TEN

While Jada and Carla disappeared for talks with Dr Robinson, Nathan stayed close to Lucy.

'Come on,' he said to her. 'Roller-coaster.'

'Been there, done that.'

He followed her into a bright study area at the front of the building which she had obviously made into her office for the duration. He sat down in a leather chair, liking the place. Lucy looked at him as if he were one of her children (not that she had any) during school holidays, then sat down at a mahogany desk.

'Shall I order tea?' asked Nathan. 'Or I could put some music on. You look a little tense there, what about a head and neck massage?' Lucy glanced at him, playfully appalled. 'You're very quiet for a journalist.'

'Just you wait until you get back.'

'It's a better story if I don't come back.'

'No arguments on that score.' She spun round. 'Do you believe all this? I mean, so you sit in that machine, it goes all psychedelic or worm holes appear before your eyes, or whatever, it doesn't mean you go anywhere. Maybe you get hypnotised into thinking you've seen your ancestors.'

'I don't know what to believe. These days they can clone a real animal out of a stem cell. What about computers, television? One minute you can be watching cricket in Australia, the next it's basketball in Utah.'

'Sorry, I just have to work this into something I can show my editor. I suppose what you said at breakfast is the best, not to think too much about it.'

'Yeah, when I get back I may say something to prove it.'

'Let's have that tea,' suggested Lucy.

'Right, where is it? Is it one of those cords you pull on the wall?'

Lucy was already on the phone asking politely for Pringle to provide tea.

'What made you decide to get involved?' she asked Nathan, hanging up the phone.

'A silly thing, really. When Jada said she felt like she was being asked to go on a vital space mission it made me think about my grandfather. His name was Stamper. That was Bruce Willis's name in the film, *Armageddon*. How stupid is that?'

'Have you chosen your three wishes?'

'I'm still thinking. Carla was funny, one minute she was going to the Second World War, the next she's back as far as she can go on her family tree to the 1600's.'

'Jada seems fixated on her doctor ancestor from the thirties and forties.'

'Whatever she wishes for she still might end up looking at a toddler playing with a doll for ten minutes. Will you listen to me? I can't believe what I'm saying.'

Lucy smiled. 'Yes, it is all very surreal.'

After a moment, Pringle knocked and entered with a tea tray. Lucy made space for him on her desk.

'Will there by anything else, miss?' asked Pringle.

'No, thank you, Pringle.'

Nathan waited for Pringle to leave. 'I heard there was to be a medical.'

Lucy checked the tea pot, then poured. 'Medical, then blood taken. Milk? Sugar?'

'Yes, and no. Blood? I'm no good with needles.'

'That does surprise me.'

Nathan smiled, accepted his cup and sat back down.

'So,' he said. 'Tell me about yourself.'

'This tea's lovely. Me? Well, I'm from Hampshire. I started on the local newspaper down there...'

'I meant are you with anyone now, since the Jackson mistake.'

For a moment she was thrown by "the Jackson mistake" comment. 'No, I'm not with anyone at the moment.'

'Can we get together after this?'

'I already said I'd be interviewing you.'

'No, I meant, together...'

'The de-briefing may be quite thorough, you'll have to wait and see.'

Nathan drank his tea in silence for a moment.

'Where do you live?' he asked.

'I live in Hammersmith.'

'I've heard of Hammersmith. It's near the Thames, isn't it?'

'That's right.'

'Hey, now, genealogy. Have you done anything of your own family?'

'My sister has started to do a few things, based on my dad's side, from the family home in Waterlooville.'

Nathan stared at her. 'Are you winding me up?'

'What do you mean?'

'You're pulling my leg. Waterlooville? There's no such place.'

'No, there is. Waterlooville in Hampshire.'

Nathan stood up, laughing. 'I'm not having that,' he said jovially. 'Waterlooville! That's like saying you come from Metropolis.' Still laughing, he put his empty cup back on the tray and headed from the room. 'Good one, that, Lucy. Good one.'

Lucy was left sitting there, dumbfounded.

***

Alone in his laboratory, Professor Pyle stood looking at his time-travel capsule. He weighed up all his previous, highly-regarded work down the years. He thought of his hard-fought reputation, of his friends and peers, of his two ex-wives in their separate Caribbean retreats. It all now rested on the contraption in front of him – was he to reach the pinnacle of his career, or fall spectacularly into infamy? He moved towards it, touched it, ran his fingers across the Union Flag paint job, made sure the Perspex hood was sealed, waved warmly at Naseby strapped into the seat inside.

'Good, old Naseby. It'll be over before you know it.'

Pyle went into the glass ante-chamber, where everything stood primed and pressured and ready to blow apart Naseby's DNA and fire it away faster than the Hadron Collider in Switzerland. Pyle's nervous eyes flicked around the dials one last time before he set the procedure in motion. Looking back to the capsule he gradually watched the capsule turn opaque. Naseby was gone.

Pyle moved around the compact room he was in. There were monitors on one wall allowing him to view the exterior of the building. Jackson was sitting alone having a private cigarette, watching a junior member of staff washing one of the Maseratis. At the back of the kitchen, a fishmonger van pulled up and Angela came outside to meet the man. Pyle hoped for some monkfish.

He looked back at the console. Then at his watch. He leant forward on his elbows.

Outside, Nathan wandered over to where Jackson was sitting on a bench. He declined the offer of a smoke. He indicated the Maserati. 'That's worth taking a picture of.'

'I've got a few.'

'Shall we take it for a spin?'

'Have you the time?'

'It seems to be the calm before the storm.'

'You're a braver man than me.'

'Or just a little crazier.'

Pyle checked everything again – the dials, the clock, what he could see of the capsule with his own eyes. His mind ticking over, he returned to lean on the desk top. Then he stood up quickly. With a resigned "oh, what the hell" kind of expression, he left the laboratory.

In the corridor, he found Dr Robinson looking for him.

'A word, please,' said Robinson.

They went the short distance back into the house proper and shut themselves into Pyle's office. Pyle, edgy and a little too attentive, sat in his place behind the desk and waited for his colleague to speak.

'Pyle, I've come to a decision.'

'Have you?'

'Before we send these people we need a more valid dry-run test.'

'Yes?'

'I'll go myself.'

'My dear fellow. That's jolly decent of you.'

'I couldn't live with myself, sending them without trying it myself.'

'I quite agree. Have you decided where to go?'

'I suppose, the furthest back that's guaranteed to be accurate - an ancestor called William Hamer from the Birmingham area.'

'Then William Hamer it shall be.'

Within two hours they were back in the laboratory, together with the technicians, returned to their posts in the ante-chamber. When Pyle and Robinson first approached the capsule, Pyle took a quick look inside for Naseby, but it was empty. When it was time, he strapped his colleague into the seat. He thought for a moment of what to say, settled for, 'Bon voyage. Remember, the nearest person to you will be the one,' then sealed the canopy lid.

Pyle walked away to be amongst his backroom staff. They performed all the necessary actions while he looked on.

Inside the capsule, Robinson listened to his heart racing while he waited. He knew what was to happen, but not the actual sensation it would effect on him. He smoothed down the trousers of his blue jumpsuit and rechecked the harness down both shoulders. Slowly the canopy in front of him began to mist over. He reached up to touch it but there was no moisture. He felt the air pressure change slightly and a calmness come over him. By then he was in the dark. He was considering whether a light need be placed in the capsule, and on a medical point he realised his heart rate had slowed and would have liked to have taken his blood pressure, when all of a sudden he felt delirium flood through him. Never being a drug user, he did not put that kind of association to the sensation, although he had tried morphine at medical school. It was an extraordinary few moments, no flashing lights, no worm holes – he was just away with the Gods.

And then he was in daylight. He found himself standing on a stone bridge spanning a moat. Slowly turning, he took in beautiful countryside with a slight mist over the ground, then he was looking at a manor house of some description, Tudor in style with smoke rising from the red brick chimneys.

'Christ, I'm alive,' he said to himself. 'Right, then. Not a soul about.' He looked over the bridge into the moat. 'William, are you down there? Have you just been murdered?'

Robinson could do nothing but stand and wait, admiring the magnificent house, part of which had the black Tudor beams, while the rest looked newer. When he was starting to become puzzled at the lack of an ancestor to look upon, he heard distant whistling. A man approached, dressed in a dark traditional postman's uniform with peaked cap. The postman stopped whistling as he stepped on to the bridge and stood to rearrange his uniform. Robinson stood absolutely agog at his obvious ancestor, William Hamer. He saw no need to speak to someone who could not hear him. Astonished that it was actually happening, he just assessed William's face and his demeanour. Then he looked down at the post that William was holding out of his bag for the big house, and was just able to read the address.

'Well, I'll be damned,' said Robinson. 'Albright Hussey. Pyle's famous Albright Hussey.'

Pleased with his appearance, William Hamer continued on to the house. A young woman in a plain dress and long white pinny hurried out to meet him. She had clearly been waiting for his arrival and they scuttled behind a wall, hidden from the house, but not from Robinson. Robinson watched them talk like secret lovers. He was surprised at how happy and emotional he was to be able to witness the little love tryst, in Shropshire, sometime in the 19th century.

ELEVEN

Zac Levy, Nathan's older brother, had two hobbies (if you counted selling novels on Kindle as a second job) – he was the star player for his local pub darts team, and was also very good at archery which he practised at a club in Cheadle Hulme.

He wondered if he could shoot arrows at the car that kept casing his house, or throw darts at the thugs when they eventually tried to come through the front door.

Seriously, he was stressed by the situation. So much so that there was a claw hammer on the hall table and he had given consideration to how fast he could get to the knife block in the kitchen.

The ex-girlfriend, who he had contacted about using her image on his latest book cover, had wanted out of her relationship. Following a series of meetings, she was now installed in his house in the Heaton Norris area of Stockport, overlooking the landmark viaduct which crossed over the town. She had also brought her two children from a previous short-lived marriage.

Her name was Stacey – at twenty-nine still the willowy blonde he remembered, if a little maturer in the face and no longer giddy. He'd had to fight someone outside Stockport bowling alley for her the first time round. Now a lot more mature himself, and protective of his expensively fixed teeth, he could do without the mounting threat from the man she had just left.

During one evening meal, he watched her across the kitchen table. She was still quite a hottie, even if her hair had lost a touch of its former teenage lustre. Great sex had resumed between them as if it had been seven months not seven years.

The children at the table were twin girls aged six; lovely little girls who by rights should have been his. Stacey had been the one to end the relationship. Zac had taken the opportunity to go out drinking with the boys and follow Manchester City (when Manchester City were crap), prepared to give her some space before winning her back. To his horror she had become serious with someone else, and before he knew it she was married to the guy.

So, there she was – Stacey. Zac decided to ride out the trouble that was brewing. A few months might find them living in peace and harmony, a proper little family.

That night his car was torched on the driveway.

***

A disoriented Dr Robinson expected to find himself back in the laboratory. Instead, he realised he was in the middle of a football pitch, with crowds in the stands shouting and chanting. Before him were the players in both red or blue shirts, apparently in a moment's pause in the action. Robinson was confused as there was no-one clearly nearest to him who could be an ancestor. He panicked slightly, thinking he had allowed himself to become trapped in a series of past happenings. He realised the crowd were not singing songs or chanting, but were in fact just cheering someone on. Robinson spun around as a male streaker jogged past his right shoulder. Cut off by police and stewards, the streaker turned back and went by Robinson on the left side.

'Who's this idiot?' asked Robinson. 'Is he another William Hamer?'

The streaker came back a third time before he was felled by one of the footballers kicking out.

***

Pyle opened up the capsule. There was no puff of carbon dioxide, just a loud squeak. To his great surprise, he found Dr Robinson sitting there with Naseby on his lap.

'Have you lost something?' Robinson asked him sarcastically.

'Naseby, old chap! Where have you been?' Pyle helped the dog and then a sweating, wired Robinson out of the capsule. 'And, Robinson, where have *you* been?'

'Pyle, I badly need a drink. You'll be very interested to hear where I've been. But I also had an unexpected bonus trip.'

'Oh, where?'

'To an ancestor with an unusual hobby.'

***

Pringle rounded up the guests for their medical examinations. Nathan followed Jada's bottom, clad in skin-tight jeans, along the corridors, while Carla was ahead trying to engage the butler in conversation.

'So, you're not married, Pringle?'

'No, madam, but it's early yet in the year.'

He was so po-faced that she was surprised by the little joke.

'You must find this all very strange?'

'I'm sure I don't have an opinion, ma'am.'

'Would you go if you had the chance?'

Pringle hesitated at the door to the medical room.

'At the drop of a hat,' he said, politely waving them inside.

Dr Robinson and two male nurses waited in the white, clinical room with three beds against the wall.

'Hello,' said Robinson. 'Please all come in. There's nothing intrusive, so don't worry about privacy. Choose a bed.'

Nathan took the one nearest the door, so in the event he watched Jada and then Carla done before him. There was a basic health check which included the taking of blood pressure. Then Pyle arrived, letting on to Nathan and Carla before sitting down beside Jada's bed. Robinson began the process of taking a blood sample from Jada's arm.

'Now, Jada,' said Pyle. 'We'll take all the specific details later, but just start to tell me about your three wishes.'

'My great-great-grandfather was a truly amazing man,' began Jada. 'He put himself through medical school pumping gas and waiting tables in Alabama. He's why I became a doctor.'

'You may not recognise him from photographs, so...'

'Oh, photographs of him were lost in a fire before I was born. That's why I'm so delighted to be seeing him face to face.'

'Just remember that when you realise where you are if you realise where you are the person nearest to you will be the right ancestor.'

'Yes, right. The person nearest to me. Do you want my other people?'

Robinson finished taking the sample and released the strap from Jada's arm.

'Go right ahead,' said Pyle.

'My second wish is to see my most famous ancestor. He was mayor in a town in Georgia. I've seen photographs; I'll know him immediately. Finally, there's an ancestor from England who interests me. They emigrated in the early 1800s. They were white, by the way.'

'Right, Jada, you rest now.'

'Yes, Professor.'

One of the nurses was already taking Carla's blood. Pyle took his chair with him and sat beside Carla. She was so keen, he just nodded.

'The first person on my list, Professor, disappeared somewhere between 1911 and 1921. She's the mystery of the family. Next, is my great grandmother. I hope I see her when she was young and vibrant. The last person is my auntie who passed away in modern times. I was estranged from her in the nineties. I wish I could have reconciled with her. She was American. A big shot business lady.'

'Okay, Carla, you rest up and I'll see you later for exact details.'

Nathan looked aghast at Dr Robinson struggling to find a vein in his right arm. 'Keep digging,' he said. 'There's one in there somewhere.'

Pyle sat down. 'Nathan.'

'This is what heroin does for you. You want my first wish? I'm not really into genealogy, but here goes. It's my great-uncle who was killed in the First World War. I'd like to take a look at him. Then, from the family tree research there was an ancestor who seems to have had three children out of wedlock, then she goes missing on all future census records, leaving her children to be brought up by relatives. I know you'll probably not be able to get to the truth but I would like to see what she looked like. Finally, the girls are probably going back to the 18th century, but I want to see a girl who died last year. She was my first love. Don't worry, she was a blood relation – my cousin.'

'Okay for now, Nathan. Remember, they won't know you're there with them. Just enjoy whatever sight awaits you. Good luck.'

Pyle, Robinson and the medics left. Pringle could be seen waiting outside.

Nathan looked at the others. 'How come I was the only one he wished good luck?'

Later in the evening, Nathan started to become very nervous, especially when Pringle delivered to his room the blue jumpsuit he would be "travelling" in. Nathan looked at the strange item of clothing, looked at Pringle's dead-pan expression, then took it from him. 'Great, thanks a lot.'

Nathan took a beer from his mini-bar, made a mental note to empty the fridge when it was time to go home, and made a few calls on his phone. He didn't get through to any of his friends or to his brother, Zac. His mother, who he had told a half-truth about why he was going away for a few days, did pick-up and they chatted for a short time – everything was fine on the home front, apart from his girlfriend Rachel phoning three times to ask where the hell he was.

There came a knock on his door. Could it possibly be Lucy? No, it was Jada.

'There's an indoor pool,' she said. 'With a bar.'

'Party?'

'Sure is.'

'Lead on.'

The pool room was made to look like a lido from an English seaside resort in the Thirties. Carla thought it delightful, but she wouldn't put on the swimming costume Pringle had provided, instead she sat by the side with a glass of wine. Jackson was playing bartender, throwing together some concoction for Nathan and Jada while they had their first frolic in the water. Nathan beached himself near to Carla and shook water from his head.

'Hey, Carla, here's some genealogy for you. My mum used to go swimming at a popular place called Sharston baths. Then the council sold it and they knocked it down to build flats nobody could afford to rent. Brilliant.'

He missed Carla's reply as Lucy made an entrance in a black bikini that looked far too sexy to be borrowed. He watched her speak to Jackson, to order a drink, or was it to best show off her figure to him?

Lucy brought two cocktails from Jackson's bar and squatted to offer one to Nathan. Once he had recovered from the squatting, he thanked her and tried the drink.

'I need to ask you something,' said Lucy.

'The answer's yes.'

'No. Is it true all Manchester United fans live outside of Manchester?'

'Are you coming in?'

'In a minute. Is it true?'

'Why do you want to know that?'

'My eight-year-old niece, who lives in... (she said it very slowly) Water...loo...ville... is a bit of a tomboy. She's into football. She likes Sergio Aguero and she also likes Wayne Rooney.'

'I'm sorry, what, she likes Wayne Rooney? Is she a disturbed child?'

'Which Manchester team should she support?'

'City, of course. To answer...' He paused as Lucy slipped deliciously into the pool beside him. 'To answer your question, I know a lot of United fans who live in Manchester. That's not to say the M56 motorway isn't clogged up before a game with all the fuckers coming up from Cheshire.'

Lucy enjoyed her cocktail. Somewhere in the building a switch was hit and music came into the pool house - Adele's *Someone Like You*.

'Oh, I love this,' said Lucy.

'Yeah, she's something else, that girl.'

'Nathan, tell me, are you nervous about the morning?'

'I tell you what, I'm glad I'm in a swimming pool, I've been peeing for half an hour.'

She giggled. 'Are you taking the first trip?'

'No way – women and children, and all that.'

Jada splashed them.

'Come on,' said Lucy to Nathan. 'Are we just standing here or are we swimming?'

They placed their drinks down on the side of the pool and kicked off with great hilarity. Nathan doggy-paddled while he stared at Lucy's flushed face.

'What?' she asked. 'Surely you've been in a pool with two gorgeous women before.'

'Oh, of course I have. But never with an ex-husband stood watching.'

Lucy laughed.

At that moment, Pyle made an entrance, wearing only baggy Union Jack trunks and singing along to Adele. He gave a thumbs up to Jackson, waved to Jada (who was suddenly thinking about Pete and his concubine theory), blew a kiss to an astonished Carla, and called to Lucy and Nathan, 'Room for a small one?' before bombing, with well-tucked knees, into the deep end of the pool.

TWELVE

Nathan joined Lucy in their favourite lounge. She was channel hopping on the television.

'What's on?' he asked.

'Nothing much. I was just watching a very old episode of *Family Fortunes* with Les Dennis, and this question was "when a performance finishes on stage, name something the audience shouts."' She giggled to herself. 'This bloke answered "goodbye!"' She laughed hysterically, while Nathan tried to understand what was funny. 'You should have seen Les Dennis's face. He looked straight at the camera and said "as a show finishes you shout goodbye!"'

She laughed again for a while before composing herself.

'You think I'm daft, don't you?' she said. 'What do you want on?'

'Football.'

'We're not watching football.'

She did look through the Eurosport channels for him but only found cycling, handball or skiing.

He told her, 'My mum thinks all cycling on the TV is the Tour De France, that they just keep cycling round for months on end.'

'Handball, bloody stupid. I don't suppose you like skiing?'

'I love to ski. I've not done it abroad since I was fourteen, though.'

'On the school trip? I went skiing on a school trip.'

She found an episode of *Friends* to watch. Nathan just sat there staring at her profile, with a smirk suddenly coming to his face as he reminisced over something extraordinary she had just triggered in his memory.

Hordes of schoolchildren in their dark uniforms with pale blue insignia walked across the frosty playing field towards the grim school buildings. Fourteen-year-old Nathan, with his Adidas bag over his shoulder, headed onto the playground to be faced with a mass football match with goals on the side of the gymnasium and across on a prefab building. The ball crashed against one of the many opaque plastic boards that cover the classroom windows (this is Wythenshawe, Manchester, where children don't need natural light to study by) and then was swamped by the enthusiastic players. Nathan's best friend, Neil Johnson, joined him and encouraged him to get into the match.

'Come on,' said Neil, 'It's fifth form against the rest. We'll join the suicide defence.'

They headed to the prefab goal, where boys their own age were packing the area, determined to keep out the older boys.

Shots rained in. Dale, a gangly boy who chose to specialise in goalkeeping to mask his shyness, called, 'Dale's!' He caught the ball. 'Out! Out!'

Everyone ignored him. The ball soon came back. Neil made a good clearance and was heartily congratulated. Dale came out for another ball, 'Dale's!' He missed it, cart-wheeled in the air and landed on his head on the concrete. Everyone ignored him and carried on playing. A large fifth former controlled the ball and fired in a massive shot which cannoned off a passing girl's head, flooring her with broken glasses and buckets of tears. A huge cheer went up. The laughing fifth former had no sympathy for her, 'Get off the fucking pitch! You silly little cow!'

Nathan and his friend collapsed into hysterics. He and Neil moved aside to catch their breaths. Nathan felt something wonderful press up against him. It was his Caroline McAlister, all fresh and blonde, her skirt folded up higher than when she left her home that morning.

'All right, Nathan?'

'Yeah. Hiya, Caroline, good to see you.'

Then she was gone, swept off by her in-crowd group of girlfriends. Neil stared longingly after her, before a disturbance took their attention. A group was moving away from the football and heading to the rear side of the gym, which meant one thing – fight!

By the time Nathan and Neil got there it was all over. They might have guessed it would involve their friend, Tony Willis. Black lad, Tony, had just despatched an older opponent, and was already being feted by all and sundry as he came away from the scene. Tony saw them and winked.

Neil said to Nathan, 'We're sorted now. Tony's just become cock of the school.'

It was a normal school day. Nathan, Neil and Tony were joined by the fourth musketeer, Glyn Carr, to be bored by Maths, baffled by double French, sit talking through double Physics because Mr Jameson had given up on the world; then it was Games. PE teacher, Mr Derbyshire, was always late, so as they queued outside the gym, they could watch Caroline and her friends making a mockery of netball.

Mr Derbyshire arrived in his track-suit with the whistle around his neck, flirted with the Girls' teacher, Miss Phelan, then approached the boys, taking a football from Glyn and bouncing it. Two boys at the front of the line, a Laurel and Hardy pair of geeks called Gareth and Tim, were mumbling their unhappiness.

'What's wrong with you two?' asked Mr Derbyshire.

Gareth ignored a threat from Glyn, before speaking to the teacher, 'Sir, it's always football.'

'What would you like to do, Gareth?'

'Table-tennis would be nice, for a change, sir.'

Mr Derbyshire looked at him askance, then clapped his hands together. 'Right, you lot. Get changed and two laps of the field. In you go.' Mr Derbyshire stopped Tony and said to him, 'I believe congratulations are in order.'

Later, upstairs in the gym, Nathan came away from the frantic basketball game to take a breather. He opened one of the small windows for some fresh air and looked out into torrential rain. Right in the middle of the field were Gareth and Tim, trying to play table-tennis.

It was that day that Mr Derbyshire gave the boys their forms for the upcoming skiing trip to Italy, which they had to take home to be signed. The four musketeers decided to head to Nathan's house straight after school, because his mum would need the most persuasion to put pen to paper. Normally, Nathan would cross the road when it came to passing the boys from St Thomas Aquinas school, who were gathering for their buses. But with Tony along, the four of them decided to go straight through the mass of maroon blazers.

'Come on,' said Tony, 'We'll intimidate the bastards.'

They were big lads, these Thomas Aquinas, thought Nathan, as somebody spat on the side of his face. Glyn and Neil were similarly treated behind him. Then from the windows of the top decks of two buses, catching all four of them, came a downpour of sputum that virtually drenched them. Tony took it in good spirit – even he wasn't daft enough to start throwing punches when outnumbered 200 to one. They got free of the mass of maroon and kept on towards Nathan's house.

Neil was horrified. 'They gozzed all over us! They gozzed all over us! What am I going to tell my mum?'

***

They landed at Genoa airport.

'Yeah, so why did we land here and not Milan?' asked Glyn.

'Did you not hear the captain?' asked posh Adrian, who was clearly in the wrong school. 'There's fog at Milan.'

Glyn was about to knock Adrian out, when Mr Derbyshire and Miss Phelan arrived on the scene. Mr Derbyshire counted heads, then turned to two fifth-former girls who were along as chaperones. 'Who are we missing?'

Adrian grassed up Nathan and Tony. Glyn wanted to hit him again. Nathan and Tony came sauntering over, eating sandwiches from the terminal.

'How did you get those?' asked Mr Derbyshire. 'I've not given you your money yet. Never mind, I don't want to know.'

They had a long coach journey, which inevitably led to a chorus of "we're in the self-preservation society" as they hit the mountain roads. It was pitch dark, and they were shattered, when they pulled up in front of their hotel in the town of Madesimo, close to the Swiss border.

Mr Derbyshire threw a suitcase to Nathan.

'Sir, I don't think this is mine.'

'It is now.'

In the hotel dining room, crowded with schoolchildren from all over England and Wales, Nathan was enjoying his continental breakfast. Neil and Tony joined him. Tony looked faintly ridiculous in his all-in-one red ski outfit and mirror shades, but Nathan kept his opinion to himself.

'On the floor above us,' said an excited Neil, 'there's a girls' school from Hampshire.'

'Where's Hampshire?' asked Nathan.

'What does it matter where Hampshire is?' asked Neil, aghast. 'Girls' school!'

Tony sat down. 'Mr Derbyshire says we'll be allowed out at night.'

'That's because he wants to spend time with Miss Phelan,' Neil told him.

'Will we get to the top of the mountain today?' asked Tony.

'I doubt it,' answered Nathan. 'Nursery slopes first.'

Someone bumped into Nathan's shoulder in passing. He looked, and saw a pretty blonde girl with a tray, apologising.

'No problem,' he said to her.

'That's one of the Hampshire girls,' said Neil.

Because Mr Derbyshire had taken them to a dry ski slope several times at home, they were only on the nursery slopes for a morning with the Italian instructor. Then, with Mr Derbyshire, Miss Phelan and four older girls, they all went up on the drag lift to the first stage of the mountain. Mr Derbyshire did notice that Tony and Neil didn't get off at the right place, continuing on higher, and he determined to carpet them for it later in the day.

Nathan stayed close to Glyn, and they both found real skiing to be absolutely fantastic. Apart from a few falls, they were quite proficient and went up and down more than most. Posh boy, Adrian, seemed a natural, though, flying past them in the tuck position, and completely winding up Glyn.

Nathan thought he recognised the pretty blonde from the Hampshire school, but he couldn't be sure on the busy slopes.

He met her again in the hotel on day three. She was in reception with her friends watching their teachers make a complaint about someone taking a dump in their communal bath tub. She smiled at him, he smiled back.

He checked with his friends about the bath tub joke, but they were all so puzzled that he knew they were innocent. They enjoyed skiing again the following day, going to the top of the mountain with strict orders to follow the person in front. Coming down, completely exhilarated even after a mad fall, Nathan realised he was skiing amongst the blonde girl's friends. Then there she was, taking a breather, leaning on her ski poles, all flushed in the cheeks. Nathan snowploughed down to her, wishing he knew how to stop parallel.

'Hi,' she said. 'Having fun?'

'I love it. I don't want to go back home.'

'You're from the Manchester school downstairs, aren't you? I'm Lucy.'

Nathan had never met a Lucy before. Fantastic, he thought, trying not to look at her pert bosom above her all-in-one outfit.

'I'm Nathan.'

She actually offered a handshake – again, something unknown to Nathan.

It was at that point that Adrian, coming down in great sweeping arcs, was homed-in on by Glyn (a work of pure genius, really) and completely wiped out! Nathan actually felt sorry for the lad.

'They'll have to get the blood wagon out to him,' said Lucy.

'The what?'

'It's a stretcher on skis. They'll take him to the medical centre.'

'Listen, would you like to do something tonight? We're allowed out.'

'I don't know. But, we're going down a toboggan run, and then having pizza. Why don't you tag along?'

'Sounds great.'

They agreed to speak again in the hotel to settle plans, then they said goodbye and Nathan skied over to see if Adrian was still alive.

It was not exactly the Cresta Run, but watching through the mass of Hampshire schoolgirls at the top, Nathan thought it looked pretty scary and radical – especially for a first date. Lucy was alongside him. Although they were both wrapped up in four layers of clothing, he felt a thrill whenever she brushed against him as she encouraged her friends to go off into the floodlit tunnel on their toboggan.

'I will follow you down!' she called to one nervous girl, then laughed and took hold of Nathan's arm.

Nathan had politely been introduced earlier and been accepted by Lucy's two supervising teachers. One of them turned and waved them over. Apparently there was such a thing as a tandem toboggan. It was almost too much for Nathan, to be expected to ride down in contact with the gorgeous Lucy, but she encouraged him to mount the thing first. Then she virtually sat on him and they inched forward until gravity took them downwards.

It was brilliant fun, the ride as well as holding her with his forearms around her waist. It went on for longer than he expected, then they came to the end and tipped up sideways, laughing their heads off.

He didn't mind that she was engulfed by her happy friends, but she came back for him and, after the teachers had counted heads and shepherded them onwards, she took his hand for the walk into town. They sat together for pizza and Seven-up. She didn't say anything about her home life, and he failed to mention Manchester; it was not needed in their brief little holiday romance. Before they parted on the "out of bounds" stairs to the third floor, they kissed for quite a long time.

After Mr Derbyshire was consulted, Nathan was allowed to ski with the Hampshire children the next day. He had to endure a little banter from the lads outside the hotel after one of the sessions, and when Tony started a mass snowball fight, Nathan fought for the girls' school.

The following day, Nathan and Lucy went through the routine of dressing and booting-up, collecting their skis and following everyone else to the first ski lift. They lingered around chatting, even assured one of the teachers that they would definitely catch the next chair. When they were finally free to hide themselves in the mass of strangers from the other schools, they waddled back to the hotel, dispensed with their skis and boots and ran upstairs.

They lost their virginities to each other in the bed of geography teacher, Mrs Dawson. Afterwards, all hot and flushed, pushing the heavy duvet from their faces, Nathan said, 'Go on, then.'

'Go on what?'

'Tell me I was great.'

Lucy screamed with laughter and they rolled about under the

cover.

THIRTEEN

Pringle maintained a small office next to the kitchen. Sitting at his desk, he could see on a monitor that the two female guests were down to breakfast, but the Mancunian was not, so had dispatched a maid to wake the man. He looked back at the American woman and the Londoner, sitting eating bacon and eggs in their blue jumpsuits. In his professional capacity, he was thinking about egg stains being transported back into the past, while personally he envied them enormously. On his computer in front of him he opened a file which contained an ornate map of his family tree. Scrolling down he could look at the few photographs he possessed of ancestors great-uncle Henry in his Royal Engineers uniform, posing against a sepia backdrop of country lane in a photographer's studio in Ealing; granny Willows at home in her Romford, Essex garden just after the Second World War; various Victorian images of her parents' stark, unsmiling wedding day; some laughing cousins in the 1950s, apparently at a Butlin's holiday camp. He had normal family pictures at home, but these were the ones that really fascinated him.

He watched Nathan stroll into the breakfast room. At first, if Pringle had been asked to bet ten pounds on which one would run a mile from the experiment, he would have chosen the man. Now he liked him and wished him a safe journey. And besides, if the competition winners came back safe and well, then Pyle may look around for immediate volunteers to go as well. Pringle scrolled back up to his tree. In his direct line it was one butler, footman or groom after the other all the way back to 1768. Who would he choose to go and see?

***

Nathan joined Carla and Jada.

'A hearty last meal,' he said to them.

Lucy and Jackson walked in. Nathan looked at her, but she had her journalist face on. Jackson was taking pictures.

'Tell me I look good,' Nathan said to Lucy, indicating his jumpsuit. 'Go on, tell me.'

It was Jackson who gave him the thumbs up after taking his picture. Nathan sat down and waited to be served his breakfast. Lucy took a phone call, moving away to stand in the window alcove. Nathan watched her, thinking about the immediate minutes after the fun in the pool, offering to help her towel down on a private corridor, being playfully rebuffed from following her into the Ladies, seeing how delicate she was with her hair all plastered down to her head. There had been a little kissing, but that was all, before she left him all alone and he went to his room.

Sitting there in the dining room, he berated himself for not thinking to joke about "embarking" the following day, or his "last night in Blighty". She was suddenly sitting next to him, pouring a glass of orange juice.

'Jada's going first,' she told him.

'Typical American.'

'Then it's Carla.'

'Are you questioning my chivalry again?'

'No, I'm just telling you facts. Dr Robinson hinted that it won't be an unpleasant trip. The technical aspect of it, anyway.'

'I'm hoping the whole thing will be a breeze. You will be waiting for me when I get back?'

'Of course.'

Across the table, they saw the two women hold hands as a sign of solidarity. Nathan looked at his own hand on the table, but Lucy just patted it, said, 'Good luck,' and got up to talk to Jackson.

Pyle came for them himself twenty minutes after breakfast had been cleared away. Everyone followed him towards the newer, clinical side of the building.

'May I suggest a trip to the loo?' said Pyle.

'Good idea,' answered Nathan, heading off.

'I meant Jada.'

Jada shook her head; she was good to go. She was first into the laboratory, where Dr Robinson greeted her with warmth and a lot of confidence-boosting hand squeezing. Pyle waited outside the door to the ante-chamber for Nathan to jog back to them, then led the rest of the group in to stand watching from behind the glass partition, while he joined Jada.

Jackson snapped away with his camera at the two scientists strapping Jada into the capsule. Once she was settled, the canopy was sealed and they both backed out of the room.

It was a very tense moment. Nathan found himself close to Lucy and they shared a glance. One moment, Jada was happily waving to them, the next the capsule windscreen turned opaque. Lucy, shocked at her own nervousness and excitement, remembered why she was there and turned to Pyle.

'Professor, has she gone?' she asked.

'Yes, my dear. When she returns, the capsule will clear.'

'And then I can interview her?'

Pyle laughed through his own stress. 'Patience. We'll see how she is first. You'll have plenty of time, I assure you.'

Just to keep talking, Lucy said to Nathan, 'When are you going on the roller-coaster?'

He smiled at her. 'I'll go this afternoon, after my trip. I may need to warm down a little bit.'

In the capsule, Jada took deep breaths. She reminded herself that she was a medical professional and to keep everything focussed and level – it wouldn't do for her to become hysterical. Even so, as the darkness enclosed her, her heart rate seemed to double and she very nearly cried out to be released. Then the extraordinary elation that Dr Robinson had experienced took her over. It was just... so, so nice as she sat there. But unlike Robinson, Jada did have images, flashbacks perhaps, in front of her eyes – vast, open farmland below huge blue sky, negro adults and negro children from various long-ago times and places, then basic wooden houses, and then more farmland bathed in warm sunshine.

Then she realised she was standing, in her blue jumpsuit, disorientated, trying to focus her eyes on her surroundings. There was darkness again, and moonlight. And, she realised, flickering torchlight.

Jada gradually became aware of raised voices. She had to lift up her head. She had to be brave. There were rows of people in front of her, all dressed in white. Jada groaned - *Am I dead?* At the very least she felt claustrophobic, hemmed in and threatened on all sides. She couldn't see anything and was upset, having convinced herself that she would be able to tell where she was. What was the point of the incredible journey if it consisted of confusion and anti-climax?

She strained to look between the massed ranks of the tall people in front of her. In the moonlight they all seemed to be wearing white hats. Orange light flickered in the gaps, confusing her. At last she realised that it was fire and flame she could just about see. A block of people shifted and she made out a burning tree. Was she at a bonfire? Perhaps a college football event? The fire was a burning cross, and the voices around her were familiar and Southern and angry. Jada began to panic. She now knew she had emerged within a Ku Klux Klan meeting.

At the front of the crowd, a bound black man had a noose placed around his neck. Jada turned away horrified.

The person nearest to you will be the right ancestor.

Very slowly Jada forced herself to turn her head. The face of the person nearest to her was just holes cut into a pillowcase. Jada was absolutely distraught; she turned away and refused to open her eyes for the rest of the time she had to stay there.

Out in a corridor, Lucy waited for Nathan to exit the lavatory. In the background she was conscious of a medical crash team on standby for Jada. Nathan emerged and smiled sheepishly at her.

'I suppose it's like having your tonsils out,' she said.

'I'm scared out of my tree here, babe. What the hell am I doing?'

'Jada's due back soon. That should ease your mind.'

'Or make me want to jack it in. She might be a fucking vegetable. Anyway, just because she comes back doesn't mean I will.'

Lucy leant on the wall with her arms crossed to try to lighten the mood.

'I'm keeping my powder dry here,' she said, 'but the excitement's mounting and by the end of the week we might all be the most famous people on the planet.'

'Don't get me wrong, Lucy, I'll be getting in that thing. But don't think anyone is going to believe any of this. It will be like we said we saw aliens.'

'Maybe.'

Suddenly, a highly distressed Jada burst from the laboratory and ran past them, quickly followed by Pyle, Dr Robinson, Carla, and then the whole crash team with their equipment.

As dryly as he could, Nathan said to Lucy, 'She's back, then.'

FOURTEEN

Zac Levy's VW Golf, or what was left of it as a burnt-out shell, remained on the drive because the police seemed in no rush to look at it and give him a crime number for his insurance firm. When Zac called them again and said there were children in the house where the arson attack had taken place – they were still in no rush.

Stacey offered to pack her bags and leave, but Zac would have none of it. He told her he wasn't bothered about things that were insured and replaceable, as long as the girls were safe. After a great deal of discussion, it was decided the girls' father would have them for a few days until everything settled down.

It was a bizarre situation, having the man who had interfered with the path of Zac's life so many years ago, showing up to collect the girls. He was a normal guy in a normal saloon car, delighted to see his daughters, a little confused as to what to feel about Zac, and clearly not happy with his ex-wife's current life choices.

Zac had taken some time off work. He and Stacey, who didn't have a job anyway, found themselves alone together in the house under the unpleasant feeling of a siege mentality. Yet it brought them closer than would normally have happened in their strange, second-chance relationship. Everything seemed more highlighted and exciting. Zac, who had never forgotten her fabulous smile, marvelled at seeing it again aimed towards him, and her distinctive long-legged walk had him watching whenever she left a room ahead of him. He never for the life of him thought he would ever get that close to Stacey again.

In the first thirty-six hours they made love constantly, once while enjoying sitting in the sun in the back garden, on a patio not completely private, but the sole overlooking neighbour was probably at work, he assured her. They laughed, they drank wine, Stacey cooked a marvellous gammon meal. But they were still listening for cars braking earlier than was necessary for the junction at the end of the road. As Zac would later say to his brother – a very strange feeling indeed.

In a hire car the following day, they picked the girls up from school and went out for a slap-up meal of burgers and fajitas and balloon animals. It upset Stacey to have to drop them off to her ex-husband's new wife later in the evening. Zac embraced her as she got back into the vehicle and everyone was waving as they drove away.

Zac half-expected to find his house burned down when they got home, but clearly nothing had taken place. He spoke briefly outside with a friendly neighbour called Brendan who told him all had been quiet while he was out.

'Thanks, Brendan. I'll get that wreck moved soon.'

'Call me if there's any more trouble, Zac.'

'I appreciate that, mate.'

Zac locked up for the night, then joined Stacey in the kitchen where she was pouring the rest of the wine. When he came close she kissed him passionately.

'Thank you,' she said.

'For what?'

'Putting up with me.'

'Nonsense. What shall we do? Do you want to watch some TV? A movie?'

'I'd really like a bath.'

'I'll go and run it for you.'

'No, you won't. I'll do it. You come up and join me when you're ready.'

'Well, if you insist.'

He checked that the rest of the ground floor was secure before following her upstairs. Perhaps he was a little too early because she was still undressing in the bedroom, but even that had a rediscovered joy to it.

'Do you mind?' she joked.

He leant on the door frame. She stripped off her underwear and stood brazen for his appraisal. Of course, there wasn't the soft, perfect blending into one vision of the nineteen/twenty year old he once knew, instead there in front of him was a magnificent, confident blonde woman.

'The water's running,' she warned.

He stepped into the bathroom to turn off the taps. The water was just right. She was there to kiss.

'Will you bathe me?' she asked.

She got into the bath and Zac went through the motions of bathing her – basically a few soapy swirls around her back and some fondling of breasts, then he was stripped and in with her.

After the frenzied lovemaking, they sat in the warm water facing each other. He looked at her pale lips and the beads of perspiration either side of her nose.

'How's your sister?' she asked.

'I haven't got a sister. I've got a brother.'

'Oh, God, yes. Nathan. How could I forget Nathan? What's he up to these days?'

'Nathan's the same as he's always been. He'll never grow up.'

'Are you going to read to me later?'

'I beg your pardon?'

'Your new book.'

Zac laughed. 'Where do you think you are? Waterstones?'

'When is it published?'

'Next week. I'll show you what the cover looks like later.'

'Is there a character based on me?'

'Not really. Probably subconsciously you're part of all my female characters, one way or another.'

She just looked at him for a moment, then told him, 'I did think of you from time to time, you know.'

'Not as often as I thought about you. You must have crossed my mind, honestly, four or five times a week, every week, for fifteen years. That's a lot.'

'That's a bit creepy.'

'I know. But at least I wasn't thinking about you while standing outside your house four or five times a week. I got on with my life.'

'How many women since me?'

'Jesus, what a question. A few. None of them compared favourably to you. I always remember, not long after losing you, I was sort of seeing a girl called Charlie. What a fuck-up she was, but that's beside the point. I think she thought I was rubbish in the sack because while I was shagging her I wanted it to be over with, simply because she wasn't you.'

'Oh my God!' She laughed. 'That's a terrible thing to say. The poor girl.'

'Poor girl, my arse. Turned out she was a selfish, nasty piece of work. Cute at the time but I've seen her recently; she's really gone to pot. Absolutely fucking dreadful.'

'Well, Zac, I never had any complaints in the bedroom department with you, that I remember, anyway.'

'Do you know why? Because you and me, we were compatible. Sexually, anyway – you were always a bit of a moody cow.'

***

Pyle gathered everyone, except Jada, in his office. Nathan thought the man seemed in high spirits despite the screaming banshee incident.

'Though Jada is heading to the airport as we speak,' started Pyle, 'we must remember that what upset her was in fact what she found, not the actual experiment... experience. I hope her hysterics in the laboratory have not distressed you. Carla?'

Nathan was giggling and Lucy slapped his thigh with the back of her hand.

'I'm fine, professor,' said Carla.

'And you, Nathan?' asked Pyle.

'Sweet.'

'Good show. Shall we press on, then?'

They returned to the laboratory. In the ante-chamber, Nathan stood with Lucy, watching Dr Robinson welcome Carla with his hand-wringing technique.

'If he squeezes my hands like that,' said Nathan, 'I might involuntarily head-butt him.'

Even Jackson at the back laughed at that.

Smiling, Lucy said to Nathan, 'Not long now until your turn.'

'When Carla's gone shall we go and get some coffee?'

'Won't it go straight through you?'

'Very funny.'

Carla's journey was more like Dr Robinson's than Jada's – she saw nothing at all. 'Oh, my word,' she said, to the feeling of ecstasy that accompanied her.

She realised she was sitting, out of doors, during the night time. She immediately got her bearings and looked at the closest person to her: a young woman, sitting well wrapped-up in a dark coat and hat, and with, apparently, a scarf tied vertically around her head, under her chin and covering her ears. Still the girl was shivering with the cold. When she exhaled, her breath was visible. Carla was not cold, but she was certainly shivering through excitement. She remained unblinking and completely gob-smacked. Could that really be the mystery ancestor from the family tree? The one who appeared on the 1911 census, before vanishing off the face of the earth?

Where were they? Carla reluctantly took her eyes off the woman's face, to look around her, seeing approximately ten other women in similar garb. Carla looked upwards to a great panorama of stars, then in front of her to the reflection of... the sea! She realised that the movement in her hips was not, in fact, tremendous nerves, but the swell of the ocean. They were in a boat!

Carla looked back at the woman with admiration. What an indescribable pleasure to be able to look at an ancestor in the flesh. Carla thought it the best day of her life.

Nobody was speaking. Carla, remembering how short the window would be, tried to take in as much of the situation as possible. Her census research came back to her, where it was advised to check neighbours because they invariably turned out to be related, so she looked more closely at the other faces in the boat. Maybe they were her ancestors, as well.

But what was happening? Carla was struggling to think clearly. Maybe her brain was still recovering from being scrambled. Finally, she decided to look over her shoulder. Looming high out of the water, some distance away but still unmistakable, its three screw propellers a shocking sight - the stern of RMS Titanic.

Awe-struck, with people crying out and moaning all around her, Carla watched the doomed liner start to sink into the North Atlantic.

FIFTEEN

Lucy and Nathan stood drinking coffee on the corridor outside the laboratory.

'If Carla comes running out of there?' asked Lucy. 'What are you going to do?'

'Catch her, and run alongside her.'

Lucy smiled. Then a loud, female wailing came from the laboratory.

'Oh, good God,' despaired Nathan.

The crash team ran in with their equipment. Lucy followed, with Nathan reluctantly bringing up the rear.

Carla refused oxygen. Her distress was purely down to joy and exhilaration. She was seriously sweating, as if she'd just given birth. She reached for the hands of Pyle and Robinson, and then Lucy. She was breathless as she spoke to them, 'I don't know what to say. Astonishing feeling. Professor Pyle, Dr Robinson, thank you. Amazing experience. What I saw...'

'What did you see?' asked Lucy.

'Let's give the lady some space, shall we,' said Pyle.

'Yes, you blood-sucking leech,' joked Nathan into Lucy's ear.

'You won't believe it, Lucy,' said Carla. 'I don't believe it.'

Nathan stepped away laughing – it was his turn next. In his best Victor Meldrew impression from the BBC's *One Foot In The Grave*, he said, 'I don't believe it!'

Carla was up on her feet and carefully being led away for a cup of tea. Like a time-wasting footballer going to the far side of the pitch just before being substituted, Nathan left the lab and went up to his room. If they wanted to send him in that thing, they would have to come up and invite him all over again.

He got an hour, before Lucy knocked and entered. Nathan was sitting with some Pringle room service in the window seat, looking out at the wonders of nature.

'How's Carla?' he asked.

Lucy was incredulous. 'She witnessed the Titanic going down.'

'No!? Wow.'

'From a lifeboat, with her mystery ancestor beside her.'

'Sit down.'

'Nathan, this is getting heavy.'

'Champagne? Have a smoked thingymajig.'

'No thanks.'

'I suppose I'm going soon?'

'Twenty minutes. Remind me, who are you chasing?'

'Great-uncle John. My only relative to die in the First World War. I don't know where. Other people went through the Blitz and all that later on, but he's the only hero, so to speak.'

'Nathan, I genuinely wish you a safe journey. No last minute terror?'

'I'm all right. If middle-aged Carla can make the trip, so can I. Do you really think she was there? Or was it a mind trick?'

'She believes she was there.'

'I suppose I'll have my own opinion on it soon enough. Are we still getting together afterwards? You weren't just being a cynical journalist?'

'I promise.'

Lucy started to leave. 'You be careful out there.'

Nathan emerged from his journey having thoroughly enjoyed the brief high that accompanied it, although he'd had much better on nights out in Manchester. There had been flashes of countryside and olde-worldy farm workers, but unlike Jada, these had been contained to enclosed, green fields, typically English. There had been a brief flashback of a more modern age as well - a city, an aeroplane, but then he was on "the other side", as Carla had put it.

Nathan found he was bent forward looking at the legs of his blue jumpsuit. He had to think hard to decide which way was up, and clear his eyes to take in the slightly misty, cold conditions. His first emotion was one of enormous relief to have made it. Then excitement kicked in.

Straight away, he could see far across hard, frosty fields to a thick, dark-green wood. Sound nearby made him look to the right. There were several whitewashed buildings and what he thought to be antique military vehicles. Instructions were shouted and then a squad of soldiers marched into view, led by what Nathan assumed to be a Sergeant Major. Officers came next, ambling along, chatting to each other. They were all clearly British Army from around the time of the Great War.

The Sergeant Major gave an order and the squad of twelve private soldiers formed into a line facing Nathan, who was completely puzzled.

'Well, which one?' he said to himself. 'It's supposed to be the nearest. They're all the same bloody distance away. Typical.'

He continued to watch them. It was fascinating stuff, nevertheless, but he felt he was being cheated out of seeing his ancestor properly.

Slowly it dawned on him, what the soldiers were doing. He looked tentatively over his left shoulder. Only five or so feet back from him, a single soldier stood with his hands behind his back, tied to a stake.

'Oh, for fuck's sake. No.'

Nathan looked back and forth, immediately close to tears. He wanted to go to the officers, but he couldn't. He wanted to go to his great-uncle John, but he couldn't do that either. He was nauseous, disgusted beyond belief.

'No!'

Nathan watched his shivering ancestor. He was a strongly-built man. His face was a calm mask, his body only quivering because of the cold morning. The British officers gathered to witness the execution. Nathan raged where he stood, first for himself at being at that place, then he rubbed his eyes and screamed for his relative. 'Fuck me!'

Nathan managed to get a grip of himself, despite the tears still flowing.

'John. Listen, John,' he said, though of course the soldier could not hear him. 'My name's Nathan. You don't know me but I'm a friend. You're not alone, John. I'm going to tell all your family how brave you are, John. Do you hear me? We're all with you, John.'

There came the sound of rifles being cocked. Then a shouted order and a volley of shots rang out.

'No!!!'

Following his de-briefing by Pyle and Robinson, Nathan walked with Lucy in the grounds of the estate. She took hold of his hand. He was still very upset. Lucy didn't know what to say.

'I feel enormously proud,' he said to her. 'It's welling up in me.'

Lucy started to cry. They stopped and stood there for a long moment in an embrace.

Dinner that evening was a sombre affair. Impatient for his dessert, Nathan found himself in the kitchen, absent-mindedly picking at a fruit cake on a plate on a counter, much to Pringle's professional chagrin, although the butler was sympathetic to the fact that the man from Manchester had just had an unpleasant trip.

Lucy came looking for Nathan. Pringle smiled gently at her before withdrawing across to the far side of the kitchen.

'Nathan, you're going again, I hear, out of turn. Why's that?'

'What? Oh, Carla's drained. Pyle suggested we wait, but I like to get on with things.'

'Are you sure?'

Then Carla entered, indeed looking tired. Perhaps she didn't want to sit with the silent Jackson as he messed with his camera. 'Pringle, I'm just after more tea.'

'I'll bring some through, madam.'

Carla reached out a comforting hand to Nathan, and then the three guests made a move to return to the dining room.

'Pringle,' said Nathan. 'I'm off again soon. Would you like to take my place?'

Pringle clearly would like that very much. Instead, he gave the diplomatic reply, 'Very kind of you, sir, but, no, thank you.'

'Top man, Pringle.'

At the dining room, Lucy let Carla go through, before pressing herself up against Nathan. 'Still nervous?'

'Yep.'

'At least the actual journey proves to be quite easy.'

'Pleasant, in fact.'

'Who are you going after this time?'

Nathan assessed her closeness to him. 'I do like your interview technique, you know. Apparently, an ancestor who abandoned her children. That's what it looks like on all the census returns.'

'Where was she from?'

'Hulme. That's an area in the centre of Manchester. Dreadful place, and that's now I'm talking about.'

Lucy smiled at him.

Later, over coffee, Pyle came in to the dining room to tell them there was a minor glitch in the system, and as a result their next trips would be put back until the morning. So, they could relax; perhaps watch a brand new movie in his small cinema, go out to a local pub, or just "chill", he actually said, around the house.

'Glitch,' repeated Nathan, after Pyle had smiled and withdrawn. 'That's an interesting word.'

'I'm trying not to be too concerned,' said Carla. 'It's no doubt an amazingly technical thing they're managing to do here. The first time went okay. There are bound to be a few gremlins.'

'Gremlins,' said Nathan. 'An even better word.'

'Well, I don't want to go out anywhere,' said Carla, rising from her chair. 'I'm just going to relax tonight. I'll see you all in a bit.'

She left the dining room.

'A local pub?' asked Lucy of her two favourite men.

'Nah,' answered Jackson.

'I wonder what films he's got,' said Nathan. 'I'm up for a big film. A bit of action. Explosions and car chases.'

Lucy pulled a face. 'Does it have to be a man's film?'

'Oh, yes,' said Nathan. 'I bet you, though, Pringle won't be able to stretch to popcorn.'

***

In the morning, for some reason, both Nathan and Lucy rose early and had breakfast together. Lucy had chosen to suffer a Jason Statham movie the night before, declining to join Nathan on the back row. In fact, it had reminded her of a family cruise on the P&O liner *Oriana* when she was a teenager, escaping the variety show and ending up watching a film with two other people spread equally around the little cinema.

Nathan paused over his porridge to check out her green combat trousers and flimsy black top with two thin straps going over both firm shoulders. Her hair was in a ponytail and she was yet to apply any make-up. He noticed a small, round scar just below her right collar bone.

'Is that a journalistic bullet wound?'

'No, it's a university disco deliberate cigarette burn.'

'Rough school.'

She ummed as she reached for the orange juice.

'So what are we going to do with our time before Pyle gets his act

106

together?' asked Nathan.

Pringle provided the answer when he politely interrupted.

'Excuse me. Mr Levy, you have a visitor at the main gate.'

SIXTEEN

While eating a Danish pastry, Lucy allowed Nathan to drive her away in a buggy. She pointed him in the direction of the main gate.

'You haven't asked me who I think it might be,' he said.

'You would have told me if you knew. I am intrigued, though.'

'I don't know anybody down here.'

They twisted and turned through the woods until they straightened out for the final leg towards the ornate gateway with its imposing Victorian gatehouse. Nathan could see Rachel Ikin's Fiat Cinquecento sitting there.

'Nice wheels,' commented Lucy.

Nathan parked up a little short and walked over alone to meet Rachel through the black wrought-iron railings.

'Hello, Rachel. This is like when I was in that open prison.'

Lucy sat and watched. She assumed the woman was a girlfriend. It was probably a silly, meaningless visit – she looked vacuous enough. Lucy brushed crumbs from her lap. It was lovely and quiet out there in that part of the grounds.

Nathan soon headed back to the buggy, with the Fiat leaving in an angry cloud of dust.

'The Manchester girlfriend?'

Nathan decided not to elaborate on his complicated love life. 'Yes.'

'Brief visit. What did you tell her?'

'About you?'

'No, you fool, about what's going on?'

He grinned. 'With you?'

'Nathan.'

'I said I was surprised to see her. My mum told her where I was.'
'And?'
'I told her all about the time travel experiments we were doing.'
'And what did she say to that?'
'It was something along the lines of "you're a mental!".'

Lucy laughed. Nathan headed them back in the direction of the big house. It was slow going at 2 mph.

'She's very pretty, Miss Manchester,' said Lucy.
'I suppose so.'
'Did she not say anything else?'
'She said my brother's in some sort of trouble. He's back with an old girlfriend called Stacey. That's a shocker; she was from the early, early days. I'm going to see Pyle straight away. I need to get home.'
'Oh, right.'

He sensed her thinking. 'You want me to finish the project first?'
'I don't know. I don't know what's wrong up in Manchester.'
'I'll come back. Lucy, this is amazing what's happening here. But it's family from the past. This is family from now.'
'Of course, you're right. I'll come with you to see Pyle.'
'If you want.'

They failed to find Pyle in his office or the laboratory. They tracked him down to the rear of the building where he was talking with one of his gardeners. He listened intently to Nathan's problem, and was understanding, but of course wanted Nathan to see out the experiment first. He even offered to send some of his "people" to deal with the situation.

'That's very good of you, professor,' said Nathan. 'But I'd prefer to deal with it my way. If you could get me to Manchester, and provide a car, I may not be away too long.'

'Very well. But Lucy, you must go too. Stop our man Nathan here from doing anything silly.'

'Me?' asked Lucy. 'All right, I suppose.'

Nathan smiled at her. 'Beirut, Tripoli, South Manchester.'

Pyle said, 'But, Nathan, before you go, there's something I want to show you. Might convince you to hurry back. Would you follow me, both of you?'

Intrigued, they went after Pyle, past the kitchen windows, through an archway and across a cobbled courtyard. Pyle disappeared into the shade of a large building, beckoning them to follow.

Once inside, after his eyes had adjusted, Nathan found himself in motorbiking heaven. There must have been twenty machines lined up – a Harley Davison, a Suzuki Hyabusa! 'Hello there!' he said. 'Professor, what part of your life isn't perfect?'

'Nathan, here we have a Ducati Supermono.' Then for Lucy's benefit, because she looked less than thrilled at the collection, 'One hundred and forty miles per hour top speed.'

Her eyes glazed over, 'Really?'

'Over here, Nathan, we have a 1960 Triumph Bonneville...'

'Oh my God,' said Nathan.

'You can ride any of these, young man.'

'I'll go and pack,' said Lucy, but wasn't heard in the excitement.

Nathan packed lightly and quickly and caught up with Lucy, who briefly attempted to explain what was happening to a concerned Jackson, then they were away in a Pyle helicopter with Damon Julius, heading for Manchester airport.

On the ground in Manchester, with a black Maserati drawn up waiting, Nathan put an arm on Damon Julius's shoulder.

'Damon, we'll go on without you from here, mate.'

'I'm under orders to stick with you.'

'Just say I outwitted you.'

Damon smiled. 'Are you sure? I'm not just a gofer, you know. I'll be there if things get heavy.'

'Three's a crowd, if you know what I mean.'

'Oh, okay.' He looked at Lucy, then handed Nathan a business card. 'I'll be waiting. Call me when you've resolved the matter.'

'Thank you, Damon.'

Lucy smiled at Damon, then playfully went towards the driver's door until Nathan chased her away like a scolded cat. 'Get in there, woman.'

Nathan settled into the leather driving seat and started the engine. He looked at Lucy next to him, buckling up. 'Any idea how to get off Manchester airport's apron?'

They found a way, emerging from Terminal 2, and Nathan took her the scenic route through the middle of the Woodhouse Park estate.

'Let's go to my house first. We can, you know, eat something, have a wash, change clothes. You can see if you want to relocate up here. Get a job with the Manchester Evening News.'

'Where does your brother live?'

'Ten minutes away, down the motorway.'

'Ring him.'

As they parked on the road, Lucy assessed Nathan's house. It was a new-build, which meant everything was on the compact scale (the garage takes a car, as long as you don't expect to be able to get out of it).

'We're home,' said Nathan, throwing a glance at Mrs O'Neil's house over the road.

Lucy used the bathroom while Nathan made some coffee and sandwiches, which he put on the table in the lounge. Because the place was so silent, he put the television on. Then he called his brother's mobile, had a brief conversation without getting round to the crux of the matter and set up a meeting for the following morning.

'Why not tonight?' asked Lucy when he informed her.

'He's at Alton Towers theme park, don't ask me why. He's not back 'til late.'

Lucy chose a sandwich and settled down on the sofa to watch an episode of *Man vs. Food*. Nathan pulled a face at what was on the screen, before sitting down, very close to her.

'What are we doing tonight, then?' he asked, cheekily.

'*Coronation Street*'s on tonight.'

'After *Coronation Street*.'

'I might wash my hair, if that's all right.'

'Of course it is. Shall we go out?'

'Maybe. Look at the size of that burger he's about to eat.'

Lucy stopped teasing and looked Nathan full in the face. He moved a breadcrumb from the corner of her mouth before they started kissing. It quickly became intense, until she stopped him.

'It's not the right time,' she told him.

'Why's that?'

The door bell rang.

'Told you, not the right time.'

He stood up. 'Don't you leave the city.' He went to investigate who his visitor was. It was Mrs O'Neil, his occasional lover, from across the road.

'What's your game?' she asked warmly, indicating the Maserati.

'You're a bit outside your comfort zone, aren't you, crossing the road? As a matter of fact, I've joined the Jehovah's Witnesses.'

'Have you now?'

'I can't explain at the moment. It's just a flying visit. Text me...'

'I texted you last night. You didn't reply.'

'Oh, I'm sorry.'

'Is there someone else, Nathan?'

'There always is someone else.'

'I thought as much.'

She leant up for a kiss, then smiled and headed home, giving him a little covert wave.

'Laters,' he called after her. He returned to Lucy. 'It was just a neighbour checking up.'

'Let's do something,' said Lucy.

'Now, that's more like it.'

'No. I mean, show me Manchester.'

He looked at her as if she were mad. 'O...kay.'

He drove her into the centre of Manchester, without bothering to point anything out to her – the monolithic glass Beetham tower was the only thing of any note. Up onto the Mancunian Way, she at least had a view out over the city centre, then they hit east Manchester. Nathan laughed – he was going somewhere close to his heart in a Maserati, with a beautiful woman alongside him, pretending he was from Argentina, that he lived in posh Alderley Edge and that his other car was a Bentley Continental GT.

'What are you smirking at?' Lucy asked.

'Can you see that?'

She glanced above a plethora of newly-thrown up little houses which were deliberately painted different colours to avoid creating a ghetto, to see the sloping grey roof of a football stadium.

She sank back into her seat, pretending to be crestfallen. 'I don't know what to say.'

'Magnificent, isn't it.'

'Will they let us in?'

'Well, although in my head I'm pretending to be a player, no, they won't. But just look at it. I'm taking you to the shop, buying you a souvenir.'

Now Lucy laughed. 'A souvenir? A souvenir of what?'

They turned down Ashton New road and drove straight to the Etihad Stadium, then turned into the car-park, parking outside the City Store, just across from the stadium.

Nathan took his time locking the Maserati, with several City fans wandering about who might happen to notice him. Lucy had to admit, up close, the stadium was pretty impressive. They entered the shop, which was always busy and began to browse. There were current shirts, both home and away, various leisurewear with the City badge, plus nostalgic items and merchandise. Nathan offered to buy her anything from a City coffee mug to a sky-blue baby-gro. Lucy smiled. She was pleased to be out shopping with him in Manchester. She pointed out a "why always me?" Mario Balotelli tee-shirt.

In the end, she settled for the City mug, a beanie hat with the club logo and a junior shirt, with Aguero letters stencilled on to the back, for her tomboy niece in Waterlooville.

It was late afternoon when they got back to Nathan's house. He asked if he had to feed her again before they went out. She looked in his kitchen cupboards.

'Obviously,' he said, 'I've not had much chance to do any shopping.'

'Let's have soup.'

He found some sesame seed and poppy breadsticks in his bread bin that were still in date. 'Cool, gourmet.'

Nathan showered first. He drank a couple of bottles of Stella while he waited for Lucy to get ready. With the limited wardrobe brought up from Surrey, she still looked casually sexy in skin-tight faded jeans and a cardigan over white tee-shirt. He complimented her on her hair and make-up.

She let him hold her hand on the five minute walk to his local pub. It was a big, lively place with customers sitting outside. There were bullet holes above the door, if you knew where to look. They were accosted as soon as they entered by friends and acquaintances of Nathan; some gave a manly welcome that totally ignored the female with him, others were genuinely courteous to Lucy and made her feel at home. The music happened to be Paul Weller, not too loud, there was pool being played and food being served at the far end of the room. As Nathan was served at the bar, Lucy heard someone talking loudly in a nearby group.

'I tell you, on my life, I was watching tennis on the telly, with British Gas digging up the pavement outside my front window. After every little bit of digging, the workman wiped his hand in front of his face and this small child ran to him with a towel.' There was uproarious laughter. 'No, seriously, I'm telling you the truth!'

Lucy asked for red wine. People near them drifted away, revealing the man with the loud voice, addressing a mixed group of men and women.

'Elvis, keep it down,' said Nathan.

Elvis looked with mock annoyance, and then his face lit up. 'Nathan!' He turned his attention to Lucy. 'I know you. I've had dreams about you.'

'Have you?' asked Lucy, grinning.

'What are you doing with him when you could be with me?'

Lucy laughed. Elvis had sunglasses on top of his head and some kind of paisley cravat at his neck. She felt Nathan's hand on her waist as he offered her glass to her.

'This is Elvis,' introduced Nathan. 'Everyone loves Elvis.'

'I love him already.'

'Elvis, this is Lucy.'

Elvis took her free hand. He had a serious expression on his face. 'Lucy, can I tell you something?'

'Of course you can.'

'I think I'm going to learn how to do a back flip.'

She spluttered, 'What?'

'A back flip. I've mastered juggling; now I want to learn how to do a back flip. You know, I can walk into a nightclub and say "stand back, stand back, clear the floor", and... ay-up, here we go...' He pretended to start the action of a back flip, then laughed, with Nathan and Lucy joining in with him. 'It'll be a great party trick. I'll be known for that instead of my fantastic looks.'

'No,' said Nathan, 'You'll just have five hundred people stood there watching you and they're all thinking "what a prick." '

Elvis gave Lucy a sympathetic look. 'Lucy, are you sure, girl? Nathan Levy?'

'I was pretty sure until I met you.'

'Where are you from, tell me?'

'London, I suppose.'

'Can I come and visit? You could take me to one of the big clubs. I was in a club last night. My mate was trying to get off with this blonde French air hostess. But every time I tried to speak French with her she just wanted to speak English. After an hour I told her she was just taking the piss and she probably came from Bolton. Her friend was scary. She said her name was Beatrice and she was a Medium. "That's funny", I said, "I had you down as a large", and backed away quick.'

He laughed hysterically at his own story.

Elvis was required elsewhere in the pub. He apologised to Lucy and let himself be led away by a girl. Lucy turned back to Nathan and sipped her wine.

'Are all your friends like him?'

'There's no-one else like Elvis.'

They listened to the music. She was not unhappy with him being pressed up against her at the bar.

'Professor Pyle would like Elvis,' she said. 'Shall we take him back with us?'

'Elvis might mess up the whole known universe.'

They chatted there together for quite a while, interrupted one or two times by someone saying hello. He offered to beat her at pool the way he had destroyed Jackson at snooker, but she declined and, with fresh drinks, led him to a free table.

'What do you think your brother will say tomorrow?'

'I'm not sure. He's so boring, usually. That's why I was keen to get back here.'

'He will open up to you, though?'

'Oh, yeah, no doubt. If he doesn't, I'll beat him up.'

She laughed. 'Doesn't that defeat the object of being here?'

Two hard looking men in their fifties entered the pub. They were welcomed with deferential handshakes, polite nods, or people just getting quickly out of their way. Nathan excused himself to Lucy, got up and went straight over to them as they reached the bar. On seeing Nathan, they laughed and smiled, one of them even hugged him. Nathan insisted on buying their first pints, despite their refusals, then they chatted for a few moments.

Nathan left the men with handshakes and returned to sit back down with Lucy. He didn't say who they were and she didn't ask. Nathan indicated people nearby starting to play darts.

'And I categorically draw the line at darts,' she said.

'No, they have a big darts competition in here each year. Look at the honours board up on that wall.'

Lucy strained to see. 'Jeff Milkins.'

'Above him.'

'Oh, cool - Zac Levy.'

On the walk home, Lucy was treated to some of Manchester's famous rain. Letting Lucy in through his front door, Nathan was pleased that the Maserati was still there. Her hair, partly ruined by the cloudburst, was made worse by him trying to rub it with a towel.

'Get off!' she laughed. She headed upstairs. 'I'll be down in a minute.'

'Yes, sort yourself out, woman. You're a shambles.'

Nathan used the towel on himself and swapped his shirt from one in the hall cupboard. He checked the phone, but there were no messages. He went into the kitchen and put the kettle on.

Lucy returned to him before the water boiled, wearing grey leggings and one of his sweaters. She leaned into his chest for a long hug.

'Nathan?'

'Mmm?'

'It's not the right time.'

'You like that saying better than I do.'

'It's not the right time, here, tonight. With what we've left unfinished down in Surrey and with what we've got to do tomorrow. I want you, in Hammersmith, when we're both relaxed and stress-free.'

'Okay.'

'Do you understand?'

'I'll go and sort out the spare room. You can make the coffee.'

'It's a deal.'

He kissed her forehead and left the kitchen.

SEVENTEEN

While Nathan and Lucy were away in Manchester, Pyle and Robinson managed to sort out their technical glitch. Unfortunately, two more problems arose immediately, with the arrival by helicopter of the first Mrs Pyle and their daughter, Adelaide.

Pyle saw his ex-wife and daughter arrive on a monitor in his office and despatched Pringle to meet them at the front door.

'Pringle, where is the bugger?' asked Lynette Pyle.

Pringle gave the diminutive harridan, who he had always disliked, a hand out of the buggy. He noticed her once blonde hair was even greyer in parts than he remembered and her eyes had the cat-like look of plastic surgery. 'The Professor is tied up, I'm afraid, madam. He says he'll meet you when you've settled in.'

'I've no intention of settling in. He's up to something, I know he is.'

'Some tea, though, surely, madam?'

While the luggage was dealt with by a footman, Pringle led the two women through to the main reception room. They flopped into a sofa each.

'Pringle,' said Lynette Pyle. 'Where are these three competition winners, whoever they are?'

'There's only one still here, madam.'

'Which one would that be?'

'A lady called Carla Terry.'

Lynette looked at her daughter. 'I knew he was up to no good. Go and find him, Adelaide.'

Adelaide threw off her coat and went out. She checked her father's office first, but he had decamped elsewhere. The laboratory was inaccessible without the door code. On a corridor, she came across Jackson, and challenged him.

'I'm Jackson. I'm the photographer.'

'Photographer?'

'Yes.'

'Photographer for what?'

'For the thing.'

'The thing?'

They had reached an impasse. She assessed him as extremely cute, if not exactly the sharpest tool in the box, and he liked her long blonde hair and slim figure. Her teeth were a bit big, but he could live with that.

'Would you like to take my picture?' she asked.

'Definitely.'

'I've been travelling, though. I'll need to freshen up first.'

Like a club comedian, he said, 'I'm here all week.'

'Well, that's good.'

She started to back up the way she had come, surprised at how shy she felt – not something she normally would associate herself with.

'Who are you again?' he asked, politely.

'Oh, sorry. I'm Adelaide Pyle. The Professor's daughter.'

'Right.' They stretched forward to shake hands. 'I didn't know you were coming.'

'It's a surprise visit. I'll see you around then, as we... go along. With the thing.'

'Yes, okay.'

It was Carla who found Lynette Pyle, by accident, as she wandered around with nothing in particular to fill her time. Instantly not seeing anything her ex-husband would want to throw his fortune at, Lynette made Carla join her for the tea that Pringle had just delivered. Carla was happy to have someone to chat to and made herself comfortable.

'I'm Lynette Pyle. One of Pyle's ex-wives, thankfully. Who exactly are you, my dear?'

Carla said who she was. When Lynette asked why she was there, Carla told her about the win in the genealogy magazine. She thought it best not to bring up the subject of time travel.

'But what is there here for you?' asked a puzzled Lynette. 'It's just that old duffer's seat in the country. I don't know why he didn't invite you to his house in Chelsea.'

'We've had a lovely time here. It's been very nice.'

'Who's we? Sorry, sweetheart, to be so nosy, but it's just not like old Pyle.'

'There was Jada; she was from America, but she went home early. And Nathan, who had to pop up to Manchester to see to some family emergency. He should be back soon.'

Lynette still looked at Carla with a quizzical expression. With a shake of the head, she put her attention to pouring the tea. Adelaide came back, said she had failed to find her father, and was introduced to Carla.

'Carla's one of the lucky competition winners,' pointed out Lynette, as her daughter sat herself down and accepted a cup of tea.

'I've just met Jackson,' said Adelaide.

'Oh, Jackson's lovely,' said Carla.

'Who in the world is Jackson?' asked Lynette.

'He's the photographer,' said Adelaide.

'The photographer?'

'For the thing.'

'The thing?'

Carla said, 'Jackson's with Lucy. Lucy's the reporter covering... the thing. Lucy's gone to Manchester with Nathan.'

'Oh, I'm lost!' said Lynette.

Outside the door, Pyle lingered with Pringle. 'Have they indicated how long they're staying?' he whispered to his butler.

'No, sir.'

'Pringle?'

'Yes, sir?'

'You know how you expressed an interest in what's going on here at the moment? Well, before we push on again with our two remaining guests, Dr Robinson and I would like to send one of our... own men, first. We'd like to send you.'

Pringle's back became even more ramrod straight. 'Thank you, sir. I'd be honoured.'

'Good man. Robinson's waiting for you. Medical and all that. Can't say when your trip will take place. Got to get rid of the in-laws first.'

Pringle nodded his understanding and Pyle went in to face the music.

'Adelaide, darling. Lynette.' He kissed his daughter and ex-wife on the cheek – Lynette's despite a firm pout. 'Ah, we're having tea, I see.'

'There's none left for you,' said Lynette.

'I'll call Pringle,' offered Adelaide.

'No, leave him, darling,' said Pyle. 'I'm fine as I am.'

'Daddy,' said Adelaide. 'What's going on?'

'What do you mean?'

'You've never had strangers staying here before. And the press. It's all very peculiar. Mummy's so concerned.'

Pyle looked to Lynette. 'How is paradise, by the way?'

'What, Kensington? I've come over for Edith's sixtieth, and may stay for Wimbledon. Seeing as you ask about Jamaica, that fool next door has destroyed my jetty with his speedboat again.'

'I'll have my people look into it.' Pyle looked conspiratorially at Carla. 'I suppose we'll have to tell them.'

Carla just raised her eyebrows and continued to sip her tea.

'Tell us what, Daddy?'

***

After a breakfast from the bakery down the road, which was a new experience for Lucy, Nathan drove them to his brother's house in Stockport. On the M56 motorway, he took the Maserati up to 130 mph, as fast as his nerve allowed – speeding tickets not being his greatest concern at that moment in time. Lucy commented on the iconic railway viaduct as they passed underneath it. 'That could do with a clean up.'

They parked near to Zac's. The burnt-out VW Golf was still there on the drive.

'I'm not an expert,' said Lucy, 'but that's not good, is it?'

Nathan rang the doorbell. A smiling Zac opened the door to them, pulling his brother into a hug. Nathan indicated the car.

'An electrical problem,' said Zac. 'It's under warranty. Come in, come in.'

Stacey came out of the living room, so that all the introductions happened at once. There was a slightly embarrassed look between Nathan and Stacey as both of them remembered their one and only indiscretion when she was dating Zac the first time round.

They settled in the kitchen. Coffee was offered to the visitors, but declined. Zac and Stacey had to assume that Lucy was a romantic interest of Nathan's. Nathan was looking out to the small garden.

'So, Lucy, you're from..?' asked Zac.

'London. I'm a journalist there.'

Stacey looked at Lucy as if she'd said she worked at NASA.

'London? said Zac. 'And how's my brother been treating you while you've been up here?'

'Very good. I've met Elvis and been to the City stadium.'

In his peripheral vision, Nathan could just detect a little smirk from Stacey.

'Zac,' said Nathan, rising. 'Show me your pond.'

'The fish have all died,' replied Zac, before adding, 'Several months ago.'

The two brothers stepped out across the back lawn. The pond was well built with a large rockery behind it. There was a metal cover over it.

'Stacey's got young children,' said Zac. 'That's why the pond's covered.'

'So, you're back with her, then?'

'Looks like it.'

'And this trouble is coming from her ex?'

'Well, if you want to call it trouble – a few phone calls, which have stopped, and the car. Making the effort to bother people soon gets boring.' He indicated back towards Lucy, 'So, where did you find her?'

'Mate, it's probably a longer and crazier story than you getting back with Stacey.'

'Stacey's still a babe.'

'I can see that.'

They both started to chuckle, then laugh. Before they knew it, they were wrestling like teenage brothers again.

In the kitchen, Lucy and Stacey had actually started to get along and were chatting.

'Look at those two,' said Stacey. 'So, are you and Nathan getting serious, or what?'

'Hopefully. It's a busy time at the moment. Maybe when it all settles down.'

'I'm really happy with Zac. Hey, we might end up sisters-in-law.'

Lucy looked back out to Nathan and his brother, now both with muddy jeans around the knees. They gave up the fight and came back into the kitchen, laughing.

'Get changed,' ordered Stacey. 'The pair of you.'

Nathan and Zac headed into the hall to change trousers upstairs, when there seemed to be an explosion at the front door, glass and wood sprayed over them as they involuntarily ducked – the two girls in the kitchen screaming out.

Nathan rushed to investigate. The damage was smaller than an explosion. 'Shotgun blast!' he shouted to Zac. Then we was out through the front door. Stacey grabbed Zac, while Lucy went after Nathan.

She ended up chasing him down the street to the Maserati. A black car had roared away after firing the shot, but it was stopped at the junction by a turning furniture van.

'Nathan! What are you doing? That was a gun!'

'Get in or get back to the house!'

Despite herself, she got in and the Maserati screeched away up the road. The black car, a BMW, had made it out to the main road. Nathan got there with a skid, the way was clear, he wheel-spun after the BMW. Lucy just hung on for dear life.

The traffic was calm. Lucy felt everything happening in a whirl. They were racing down a wide road, then left through traffic lights which were green for the BMW but just turning red for the Maserati. The next stretch was downhill, and Lucy almost cried out. She could see the blue signs for a motorway and didn't want an even faster chase. A mini-roundabout slowed the BMW, left was blocked, the route ahead to the motorway was blocked, so it had to go right. Nathan had closed right up. The BMW should have gone right around and back on itself, but it went right, up a very steep entranceway to a DIY superstore car-park. Up went the Maserati, scraping all the off side on a wall. The right wing dented on a metal barrier that stopped lorries entering the car-park, then Nathan was stalking the BMW slowly though the parked vehicles. He had not said a word since leaving Zac's.

As a journalist, Lucy was unhappily imagining how it would pan out for a story. It was not going to end quietly, that she was sure of. Nathan suddenly stopped three quarters of the way up a lane and got out.

'Stay here!' he ordered.

Lucy watched worriedly as he ran forward, anticipating the arrival of the BMW outside the front of the store, and indeed it did come round and become blocked. She could see one white face in the BMW, turning to look at Nathan. Surely he was about to fire his gun again, and that meant everything – the death of Nathan, or a terrible injury to him, the police, a trial, a funeral.

Nathan borrowed a length of two by four timber, which was being pushed along by an old man on top of his trolley, and charged the BMW as if he were jousting. The wood smashed through the driver's side window. He wasn't sure if the impact connected with the driver, but the second, third and fourth thrusts certainly did.

He left the man a bloody mess with the wood sticking diagonally out of the car. Horrified shoppers stood by watching. Police sirens were to be heard in the distance. Lucy had taken it on herself to get into the Maserati's driving seat. She performed a quick three-point turn, waited for a jogging Nathan to return and jump in, then left the DIY superstore as quickly as she could manage.

He was remarkably calm, even directing her back to Zac's, where they sat parked on the quiet road.

'Was he still alive?' Lucy managed to ask.

'I think so.'

Even though he was still hyper with adrenalin, Nathan reached for Lucy's hand and she let him take it.

'What now?' she asked.

A Jaguar car pulled up. The two men that Nathan had spoken to in the pub stepped from it, and began looking at Zac's VW.

'Now,' said Nathan, 'it's in the hands of my two uncles from Wythenshawe.'

EIGHTEEN

Lynette and Adelaide Pyle still remained slightly puzzled, fairly disturbed, quite fascinated, as well as both mulling over all the financial gains to be made, as they stood in the laboratory ante-chamber, watching Pyle and Robinson strap Pringle into the capsule.

Adelaide was still in the flirtation stage with Jackson and had him alongside her. 'Do you believe this, Jackson?'

'I just about accept it now.'

'It's just astonishing. I feel quite dizzy with it.'

She touched her right cheek with the back of her left hand, but noticed that Jackson had missed his cue, so decided not to become faint.

Lynette had Carla on her other side. During all the waiting around for the technical procedures beforehand, she had listened dumbfounded to Carla's description of the last moments of the Titanic. At first she had thought the uncouth London woman to be slightly unhinged.

'Where does the butler think he's going?' she asked Carla.

'After his grandfather. Generations of butlers, apparently.'

'How grim.'

Pyle and Robinson withdrew from the chamber.

'Here we go,' said Carla. 'Should be quite quick now.'

Pringle peered out through the canopy at them all. He was thrilled to be going, although this was tempered by the institutionalised guilt of being the served for once, instead of the server.

He settled back – forget them. He loved his Family History, and here he was going back to see a snippet of it. He was so excited he realised he was digging a nail into the palm of his right hand. He gasped as he suddenly lost his sight, then realised it was the capsule sealing out the light. Undiluted joy flooded into him, lifting his cheekbones in an unusual laugh and making his eyes blink. He lost track of time.

The light came back to him in a flash. He was standing, in his usual upright posture, facing ornate panelling and tapestry, so as to immediately think he had been chewed up by the machine and spat out into his normal job somewhere else in the house. How dare he think he could rise above his station in life and experience something beyond the extraordinary?

'Pringle! What time are the Hamilton-Wards getting here?'

He turned swiftly as he failed to recognise the voice. A distinguished man with a heavy grey moustache and wearing tweed faced him.

'I'm afraid I don't know, sir,' Pringle blustered.

'Pringle, are you there, man?'

Pringle had been looked straight through. He wasn't actually there. He looked about the room, to find no-one else present. There was a mahogany desk set in front of the windows. In the bright sunshine outside, Pringle could see an antique Rolls Royce being polished by a chauffeur who wore clothes that seemed to date from the 1920's.

'And where's my tea?' called the gentleman in the tweed.

A servant in tails entered the room. He waited for the gentleman to look at him before speaking.

'My Lord, the Hamilton-Wards should be at the station within the hour.'

'Very good, Pringle.'

Pringle stared at this other Pringle. As with Nathan, tears welled in his eyes. It was a simply beautiful thing to be standing there.

'I'll go and make sure arrangements are in place to collect them, my Lord.'

'Very good, Pringle.'

Pringle watched the other Pringle leave the room. No, surely not – was that all he was going to get of the man?

Then a woman came in, a housekeeper bearing a silver tea tray, which she placed on the table.

'Thank you, Mrs Pringle.'

Pringle's eyes shot to the woman's face. His grandmother? His time would be spent with his grandmother. He watched her with the tea stuff, watched her movements in her black dress – quite a nice, petite figure. He watched what he could see of her face, pretty but firm because of hard work, and her hair put tight into a bun on top of her head, and he watched the way she and the Lord of the Manor exchanged nervous, flirtatious glances with one another.

'Will that be all, my Lord?' asked Mrs Pringle, with just the slightest trace of innuendo.

The Lord flushed slightly above his moustache. 'For now, thank you, Mrs Pringle.'

Mrs Pringle gave a little bow without lowering her eyes and left the room. Pringle said to himself, 'Well, these things took place. Well, indeed. But what did Robinson say? The person nearest to you will be the ancestor. *The person nearest to you!* My God.'

He looked back again at the man who was his real grandfather.

***

Nathan and Lucy arrived back by helicopter later that day. Nathan went straight to his room, ran a bath and ordered up room service.

Lucy had been looking forward to seeing Jackson, but she was quite put out to find him welcoming her with Pyle's daughter in tow. She was even more annoyed, in a strange way, to realise that they were clearly attracted to each other. Lucy was polite with Adelaide Pyle, who was apparently in on the secret and all keyed-up about it, and promised to speak with her. But first she feigned exhaustion and, with a peck on Jackson's cheek, cried off to be allowed to recover alone.

She went to her room and sat on her bed. She really was tired, and also emotionally drained after her Manchester experience. She was all confused over her feelings for Nathan, and she was upset with Jackson. Why, exactly, she wasn't sure; he had dated since their divorce, women had taken an interest in him, but Adelaide Pyle was major league. Lucy put it down to the stress of the moment, and picked up the phone to order a stiff drink.

In his office, Pringle sat looking at his computer. He had up on screen the 1911 census. He typed in Grandfather Pringle's name, year of birth, place of birth and occupation, and clicked the search button. Up popped a large list of people all living at the same address. Pringle moved the mouse to scroll down before he looked at the head of the household – he knew it was a well-to-do family with at least twelve members of staff. He looked at names of maids and under-footmen and gardeners, slowly bringing the page down until he saw Mrs and Mrs Pringle, high in the pecking order. Then it was the daughters of the householder – Lady This and Lady That, feckless wasters waiting for their leisurely lives to move into leisurely marriages. Then at the top of the list, Lord Bernetton, Justice of the Peace etc, etc. On another page, Pringle typed in *Lord Bernetton*, together with his lifespan, and sat back to look at the images which popped up.

He heard Angela, the cook, call him from the kitchen next door. He would look up Lord Bernetton's life story later. He went through to the kitchen, to be presented with a tray which carried a plate of what seemed to be beans and sausage on toast, and a glass of coca-cola. Pringle looked up at Angela in mild disgust.

'It's what the man from Manchester ordered,' said Angela, unapologetic.

Pringle took Nathan's order upstairs.

'Snorkers!' shouted Nathan from the bathroom as he heard the butler enter his room. 'In here, Pringle!' Pringle didn't bat an eyelid at serving someone who was sitting in the bath.

'Pringle, working so soon after your trip? How was it?'

'It was more than I could have dreamed of, sir.'

'Top man. I'm proud of you.'

'Thank you, sir.' Pringle turned to leave, then looked back. 'I wish you good luck with your next journey, sir.'

'Thank you, Pringle.'

***

Nathan found himself in a dimly-lit room facing the wall. He could hear voices. As he gathered his wits about him, he turned slightly to the left. Someone began tinkling on a piano and he saw that man first: a formally-dressed and bewhiskered person. Little girls rushed into Nathan's line of sight, wearing brightly coloured dresses and with bows in their hair. A smiling woman was setting a table for a feast.

Nathan completed the turn so that he was facing the room – full of people, smoking and drinking, some of whom, he decided, must be his ancestors. As instructed, he sought out the nearest person there and she literally walked right past his nose to join the man at the piano. Nathan stared at the female ancestor with the reputation for child abandonment, finding her fairly pretty and definitely a happy person, looked upon warmly by everybody there. Suddenly, she set off into song, putting her hand on the piano player's shoulder. Nathan looked on in fascination and delight. The song was something from the old music halls, hard for him to follow, but everyone in the room seemed to enjoy it. Nathan smiled at them all, as if he were surrounded by relatives at a modern day family function.

After that song, she was encouraged to sing another.

'Auntie Maria,' called one of the little girls, 'Do sing another one. Please.'

Maria didn't need her arm twisting to throw herself into another tune. Once more, Nathan became emotional, as he continued to look at Maria's face with tears in his eyes.

***

On her second trip, Carla also emerged into a darkened room. But this was a bedroom, with old fashioned décor and a single brass bedstead. At first Carla thought she was alone, and waited for somebody to come in, before a child stirred in the bed. Carla continued to wait and wonder, looking at the child's angelic face.

Finally, Carla realised that she was, after all, looking upon her great-great-grandmother as requested.

'As a child,' whispered Carla. 'That's wonderful.'

It was such a surreal moment for Carla. She knew her time was limited, that every second counted, but she was absolutely charmed nevertheless, happy to stand there for her allotted length of time.

Later, Carla found Lucy and Nathan crashed out in one of the lounge areas at the front of the house.

'You charlatan!' kidded Nathan. 'You fraud. What kind of a trip was that? A sleeping child. They can't use ten minutes of that when they make the movie.'

Carla sat. 'Oh, it was lovely, Nathan. So much nicer than the previous one.'

Lucy stretched to be able to pat Carla's leg – they were all getting quite close.

'So, the evening off,' sighed Carla. 'Then we have our final trips tomorrow.'

'What are you going to do tonight?' asked Lucy.

'Have a long bath.'

'Pringle!' joked Nathan.

'I'll interview you at some stage,' said Lucy to Carla.

'Okay. And I suppose I should ring my husband. He'll think I've been kidnapped.'

Nathan lightly nudged Lucy. 'When are you going to interview me?'

'I'll come along after Carla, later on.'

In his room, Nathan drank beer and watched sport on the television. A knock at the door made him jump up and check his appearance in the mirror – he was expecting Lucy.

He opened the door slowly, and found Pringle standing there.

'You again, Pringle.'

'Hello, sir. Professor Pyle has arranged a special entertainment. Could you be in the lounge in ten minutes?'

'I suppose so.'

Pringle offered blue fire-proof overalls and gloves to Nathan. 'Wearing these, if you don't mind, sir.'

Nathan raised his eyebrows, but accepted the garments.

Suitably dressed, Nathan put in an appearance in the lounge. He smirked at Lucy in her baggy overalls, but she silently warned him with her expression from making any comment. Adelaide Pyle was there with Jackson; Nathan had met her and her mother just before his trip to see ancestor Maria, and had been suitably polite to his host's daughter and ex-wife. Pyle was the only one who looked normal in his overalls. When Carla showed up, slightly late, they walked outside to waiting buggies and were driven off in the direction of the roller-coaster. Pyle had guided Nathan to join him and Carla, with Pringle doing the driving. Lucy sat in the front of her buggy with the driver, infuriated to have to listen to Adelaide and Jackson chatting away intimately behind her.

Pyle said to Nathan, 'I know we keep having interruptions to the schedule, but you really will enjoy this. What do you drive, at home in Manchester?'

Nathan thought of the damaged Maserati left behind at

Manchester airport with a disbelieving Damon Julius. 'Whatever I can get into.'

Pyle took a moment to understand that, then smiled.

'I've been driving my girlfriend's Fiat recently,' continued Nathan.

'What would be your dream car?'

Nathan gave it some thought. 'A Ferrari 430.'

'Any others?'

'The new Porsche.'

Pyle seemed slightly disappointed at the answers, but he pulled himself together as they went past the roller-coaster and rose up through the woods. Nathan became aware of a *Close Encounters of the Third Kind*-style glow emanating from the other side of the hill. The two buggies came out of the trees and stopped side by side.

'Bloody hell,' said Nathan.

Below them, laid out on an expanse of flatland, was a full-size, floodlit, oval racetrack.

'Apparently,' said Pyle, without any hint of bragging, 'it's a replica of a famous racetrack in California. Or so I'm told.'

'Bloody hell.'

Feeling tiny in the pit lane, the two time-travellers, the Professor's daughter and the Press, now all carrying helmets embossed with the Pyle logo, stood admiring two black Lamborghini Murcielagos. The track technical people and professional drivers were speedily getting the cars ready to race.

'That was my third choice,' Nathan said to Pyle, who laughed.

Everyone went round the track as passengers first, given instruction by Pyle's expert drivers. It was Nathan who was allowed to get behind the wheel first, taking Pyle with him. At an interval of thirty seconds, Jackson took the second Lambo out. He had called, 'Come on, then.' Lucy was a little miffed that he had been asking Adelaide Pyle to accompany him.

An exhilarated Nathan sped around twice, almost catching up to

Jackson, before he turned off into the pits. 'How long can we do this for?' he asked Pyle.

'All night long, if you wish.'

Carla waited nervously to take Nathan's car.

'Quick driver change,' he said, jumping out, pretending they were in a 24 hours race, but she didn't understand. 'Have fun, Carla,' he added quickly.

Carla had a track driver along with her. Nathan and Lucy waved her off.

'You next,' Nathan said to Lucy.

'Will you come with me?'

'Sure.'

They took out Jackson's Lambo, and had great fun with it. After an indulgent four laps, Lucy finally pulled into the pits. She and Nathan joined Carla to sit on the concrete wall with soft beverages and towels for their sweating faces.

'How was that?' Nathan beamed at Carla.

'That was great! I think I could have gone faster, though.'

'This one,' Nathan indicated Lucy, 'didn't want to stop.'

Lucy laughed, exhilarated. 'I got the taste for fast driving while up in Manchester.'

'Why, what happened in Manchester?' asked Carla.

'Oh, nothing,' answered Lucy, quickly. 'I just had a go in the Maserati.'

Carla took a drink from her lemonade. She looked around the amazing circuit and thought how, only a week earlier, she would have thought it ridiculous that she would be in such a place. She watched Jackson chatting with Adelaide, who was getting ready for her drive, and saw how Lucy's face dropped as she also took in the scene.

'Well, then,' said Carla, moving the conversation away. 'After this fun, it's our last trips, then back to reality. You'll be off to Manchester, Nathan? And you, London, Lucy?'

'Probably,' they both said together.

Adelaide and Jackson left in one of the Lambos with Pyle proudly waving his daughter off. He looked quite emotional, as if his daughter was off on honeymoon.

'Your husband will be glad to see you,' Lucy told Carla.

'I should think so – he's had to cook his own bloody tea.'

They all laughed.

Lucy said, 'Carla, remind me, what's your final wish?'

'My estranged American aunt. She passed away at the start of the century. It's always upset me that I lost touch the way I did.'

'And yours?' Lucy asked Nathan.

'A girl called Kezia. She was half-Indonesian. My first love. We were cousins. I know, that's probably not allowed, but she was stunning. Fresh faced, raven hair, black eyes. She was killed in a car accident. It still eats away at me quite often.'

Floodlights suddenly came on, as dusk began to settle over Surrey.

Nathan jumped to his feet, adjusted his gloves and winked at them. 'Right, then, the night time session.'

Pyle was approaching them, with behind him two members of staff free-wheeling the Hyabusa motorbike.

'Let's change the rules,' Pyle said to Nathan. 'Now you're more familiar with the track, do you think you can handle this machine?'

Nathan was speechless. He looked at Lucy – she pretended to be excited for him. In a daze, Nathan went off with Pyle's men to be changed into some leathers and to discuss how to ride the circuit on two wheels.

Soon he was lapping the 'Busa, and having the time of his life.

NINETEEN

Nathan and Carla sat in one of the lounge areas, waiting to go on their final trips. They were not particularly nervous any more, aside from his foot tapping, and her cuticle-checking. They were being kept company by Lucy and Jackson, who were on the same couch, but miles apart.

'And where's Adelaide?' Lucy asked Jackson, snidely.

He gestured that he didn't know. Then looked at her as if puzzled by her tone of voice.

Dr Robinson popped his head around the door. 'Another slight glitch, people. Maybe an hour.' He smiled apologetically and left them.

'There's that word again,' said Nathan, working the room. 'Glitch. They're fond of that word.'

Lucy smiled at him.

'Shall I put the telly on?' asked Carla.

She switched straight to BBC One's *Bargain Hunt*, where two teams compete to buy antiques and make a profit at auction.

'Oh, my good God,' despaired Nathan, as Lucy happily settled in to watch the programme.

'Are you not a fan of daytime TV?' Lucy asked him.

'I'm not a fan of daytime.'

'Go and do something, then, you've got an hour.'

'We've done everything Pyle's got to offer.'

'I know of one more place in the grounds.'

'And what would that be?'

She smiled again. 'Maybe I shouldn't say. It might be too distracting to you at the moment.'

'What does that mean?'

She just laughed.

'Lucy?'

'We'll try and get in there before we leave.'

'I can't wait.'

Adelaide Pyle passed through on her phone.

'Have you got rid of Jason Kanini yet?' she asked into the phone. 'I know you can't sack him, but persuade him to move on. I don't care... no, I don't care, just do it.'

Then she was gone from the room. Nathan looked after her with a quizzical expression on his face.

'What's wrong?' Lucy asked him.

'You heard her talk about sacking a Jason Kanini?'

'Yeah. Weird name that is, Kanini.'

'Jason Kanini's my cousin. I don't suppose there are many Jason Kanini's knocking around.'

'Probably not.'

'I'll phone him when I get a chance.'

***

Pyle's avoidance of his ex-wife had been akin to a vintage comedy film – continually moving from room to room, telling staff to cover for him and even hiding for a time at the top of one of the stairwells, where she was certain not to go. When she did track him down, it was just like the old days, haranguing him over money issues, and now, with this new invention of his, there looked to be astronomical pound signs to be discussed. He had listened to her patiently, nodding, assuring her that he was not deliberately keeping things from her or their children.

But then, the previous evening, she had found him in Pringle's office, where he was trying to enjoy a rather nice malt whiskey and scan through the Times. To his surprise, she just wanted to talk about the ins and outs of the capsule and how exactly the procedure worked – how safe it was, did it hurt in any shape or fashion, whether there were any long-term side effects. He tried to answer her questions as best he could.

Then she came out with it, 'I want to go on a trip in the capsule. I won't take no for an answer.'

'I beg your pardon, dear?'

'I intend to visit one of my ancestors.'

'But, as I said last night, it's not entirely 100% safe.'

'My mind's made up.'

'But...'

'Don't try to dissuade me.'

Pyle sat there and wondered why he would try to dissuade her. He remembered Robinson once telling him the famous mother-in-law joke - "The mother-in-law's gone to the Caribbean."

"Jamaica?"

"No, she wanted to go".

It didn't really work with ex-wives, but here was an opportunity to send Lynette Pyle farther away than he ever thought possible.

'Well, if you insist, dear.'

She was sent in secret by Pyle and Robinson, without any lab technicians present, while Nathan and Lucy waited around the house. Once she was on her way, to the short, remarkable life of her Victoria Cross-winning Coldstream Guards great-great grandfather, Robinson seemed preoccupied with something. Pyle looked at him and asked what was wrong.

'I'm just wondering where Naseby is,' said Robinson.

Two hours later, Adelaide Pyle made her presence known to all the house guests; her screeching voice following her father through the downstairs rooms as she furiously demanded to know where her mother was.

'She's not left,' stated Adelaide, 'because all her clothes are still here. And Pringle says nobody has left the estate by car. I've looked everywhere, daddy, and she's not to be found.'

'She'll show up, darling,' placated Pyle's voice. 'She must be hiding somewhere.'

'Hiding!? Why on earth would she be hiding?'

'Or wanting to be alone, darling. I wouldn't worry.'

'Daddy, I am worried.'

Four hours later she was howling onto the shoulder of Jackson in the main foyer. 'He's done her in!' she accused her father.

'Don't say that. There'll be some simple explanation, you'll see.'

'She's been missing all morning, Jackson. Ever since that problem stopped Nathan and Carla from going... Oh, my God, you don't think?'

'Think what?'

'You don't think he's sent her off into the past?'

The journalist in Jackson was loving the idea of murder by time travel, almost smirking, but he shook his head decisively and rubbed her upper arms. 'Don't be silly.'

'He's mad enough to. He has, you know. He's gone and done it.'

'Now, Adelaide...'

She was working herself into a state of high agitation.

'Maybe she wanted to go,' suggested Jackson.

Adelaide's eyes almost popped out. 'Oh, no! And now she's stuck unable to get back. She'll die horribly!'

With that she ran from the room, Jackson in hot pursuit, passing a smiling Nathan and frowning Lucy who had both heard the "die horribly" comment. Once alone, Nathan said to Lucy, 'That relationship is coming along nicely.'

Before Lucy could reply, they were both highly surprised to see a returned Jada walking towards them, with a footman carrying her luggage and Pringle closing the front door.

'Jada!' exclaimed Lucy, skipping forward. 'You're back!'

'Yes, here I am. Professor Pyle talked me into giving it another try.'

The two women embraced.

'That's fantastic!' said Lucy, as they went in, still holding on to one another's waists.

'Great,' said Nathan to no-one in particular. 'You can see about the glitch.'

Nathan and Lucy were again drinking coffee on the corridor outside the laboratory.

'Did you ask who Jada's gone after this time?' he asked.

'It's some other high-flying ancestor. The mayor of a big town. Hopefully she'll find him celebrating a big election win, or something.'

'Or catch him with an intern.'

***

Jada emerged into a very crowded seating area. She gathered herself and tried to focus. She was in an aisle. The room around her was plain. Women with big hats were fanning themselves against the humidity. Jada felt a little dizzy. She realised she must be at a show of some kind. The ladies' outfits suggested the 1930s to her.

Jada slowly turned, looking for her ancestor. He was right there, a quite distinguished-looking white gentleman, sweating in a suit and tie, chatting to a man beside him. Jada continued to try to relax, breathing deeply, while taking in her moment in time there. She was impressed with her ancestor's demeanour – he was clearly a man of importance.

Jada's ancestor made a joke to his friend. Jada laughed along, even though she didn't quite catch it. To find out where she was, Jada strained to look down upon a stage. There were props of tables and chairs, two Stars and Stripes flags hanging limply, but no people. She assumed it was the interval. She continued her staring at her ancestor.

Pandemonium ensued as a once-again distraught Jada rushed from the laboratory with Pyle and Robinson chasing.

Nathan said to Lucy, 'She's off again.'

Lucy set off to follow the little group. When she met Nathan again later outside on the lawn she told him, 'Jada's gone to the airport again.'

'What was it this time?'

'Errm, what do you call it? The electric chair. Old Sparky. Ancestor was on official business, apparently.'

Nathan squatted down and rubbed his face with the palms of his hands.

'That poor woman,' he said.

Lucy joined him and put an arm over his shoulders.

'Maybe you shouldn't go on,' she suggested. 'You might find something worse.'

'I think I'll be all right. I'm only going back to a girl from my estate. It's not bigtime charlies, like Jada's people.'

'I suppose so.'

'It's Carla we should worry about. She's going to the madhouse: America.'

TWENTY

Nathan emerged from his third and final trip. He found himself unable to fully take in his surroundings, due to the fact that he was half in and half out of the wall – an extremely distressing occurrence indeed. Of course there was no physical sensation such as pain, and he would get out of the problem as easily as he had entered it but, nevertheless, it upset him greatly for a moment or two, until he managed to calm himself down.

The sound of splashing water and steam drifting past his face took his attention. He turned his head inwardly to a dimly-lit bathroom. In the bath, her black hair piled on top of her head, her translucent skin flushed with the heat, her fabulous breasts half hidden by the rim of the tub, sat *his* Kezia – gorgeous, wonderful, in the prime of her short life. Nathan no longer cared that he was stuck in the wall, so enthralled and emotionally overcome was he, transfixed to be able to set eyes on the love of his life once more. His mouth moved as if to speak, but he had lost that power. He did very well not to cry again.

There had been a time when Nathan felt that to be with Kezia was the meaning of life itself. She was adorable. She was happy and trustworthy. She loved him "enoromously" as she delighted in saying wrongly. Being able to see her again, well, the emotion completely overwhelmed him, and he started to cry his eyes out. His baby. His lost Kezia.

***

Pyle came to speak to Nathan later, while he was sitting in a lounge area with Lucy and Jackson, recovering from the draining experience. He was now unable to stop smiling since his return. Nathan jumped to his feet and embraced the Professor, who was laughing and pleased for him.

'Pleased, then?' asked Pyle, sharing smiles with Lucy.

'Words can't express...' said Nathan. 'Just to see her again. Thank you so much.'

Nathan broke down in tears again. Lucy got up to take him from Pyle and hold him.

'Sorry about the wall thing,' said Pyle.

'Don't worry about it. These things happen all the time.'

'In the bath, eh?' said Jackson.

'Yes, in the bath,' said Nathan. 'But not getting out of the bath. Damn you, Professor.'

They all laughed, and Lucy became squeezed between Nathan and Pyle, with Jackson encouraged to get up and join in the team hug.

Now the nerves hit Carla, as she was about to go to the capsule for the last time. Nathan tried everything to take her mind off it, suggesting that he could throw together a cocktail if given the right ingredients, or that he was good at foot massages ('Don't hold your breath,' he said to Lucy, standing nearby.) or, what about a game of tennis?

'You've completed your trips,' Carla pointed out to him, 'why don't you get off home?'

'Because you haven't finished. We're a team, don't you know? Well, if you discount that quitter Jada.'

Carla was touched by his support.

The call came from Dr Robinson and she got out of her chair. There was another team hug before she led them out.

Nathan and Lucy watched her departure in the capsule from the ante-chamber.

'No more coffee,' said Nathan.

Lucy suggested getting some fresh air, so they wandered the lawns at the front of the house.

'Ah, that's a lovely breeze,' said Lucy.

'I've been thinking.'

'Thinking? Careful, now.'

'How are we going to find any time together after this? I mean, this has just been stage one. Once you report it, we go onto a merry-go-round that we can't get off, don't we?'

'We can probably fit in a couple of hours before I make the call. Don't go back to Manchester. Stay with me. Be with me when the circus starts to roll.'

'Okay.'

A Maserati was brought round to the front door. Lucy and Nathan watched the driver get out, open the rear door and then the boot. Pringle came outside, laden with luggage.

'Pringle, what's happening?' asked Lucy.

'Miss Adelaide is leaving us.'

Out flounced Adelaide Pyle, talking ten to the dozen back at Jackson, who trailed in her wake. 'I'm going to tell all the family!' she ranted. 'It's shocking, no-one cares that daddy has made mummy vanish. He's actually made her vanish! You don't even care.'

'I do care, Adelaide. Come back inside and calm down.'

'Don't you dare tell me to calm down!' She got into the Maserati's passenger seat and slammed the door. Then she opened the window. 'And you can forget about seeing me in London. Consider the offer retracted!'

She instructed the driver to go and the Maserati drove off, leaving Jackson in a cloud of fine white dust. He looked over and shrugged his shoulders at Lucy.

Lucy went over to Jackson. 'Jackson, she never seemed a nice person, really.'

'I know. It's just...'

'A bit spoilt, probably.'

'I know. It's just…'

'Once you get back to London…'

'I know. It's just, I think she was really, really loaded.' He laughed, hugged his ex-wife and smiled over at Nathan. 'Let's go and check. Surely one of the women will be coming back.'

Nathan went for a shower in his room. He was dressed again and doing his hair in a mirror when there came a knock at the door. Expecting Pringle, he finally got Lucy. 'You're here at last,' he joked.

'Sorry, what?'

'Never mind. What's happening?'

'They've still not got Carla back.'

'It's been over an hour now. Do they know what they're doing? No, don't answer that.'

'Have you got a drink in here?'

'You're joking, aren't you? I might have some coke in the mini-bar.'

He found her a lemonade and she sat down with it.

'Pyle says it's all under control,' Lucy told him. 'They're trying a few different ways of tracking the… God knows what… DNA strands that they've stretched back into time. Woah, can I hear myself?'

He squatted in front of her. 'Don't panic. Maybe she's just enjoying some extra time with her ancestor. It could all work out great. She might have missed something exciting if she'd come back in the normal time.'

'I hope you're right.'

'What else did Pyle say?'

'Errm, he said, when all else has been explored, they could still send you along after her to pop out and take a look around.'

Nathan was flabbergasted. 'That's good of him.'

An hour further along, with Nathan making sandwiches in the kitchen under the gaze of Pringle, Carla was still to return.

'It's getting really bad now,' Nathan said to Lucy, who was leaning against a counter. 'What if they can't get her back?'

'They will,' said Lucy.

Nathan plated up a cheese and pickle sandwich and handed it to Pringle – the butler being too worried to follow protocol any more. Pringle nodded his thanks and left the kitchen. Nathan turned back, to find Lucy had moved in for an embrace. He clasped his hands along her lower back and spoke into her delicate neck. 'You're amazing, you know. Beautiful, talented, dedicated, a little odd to be working with your ex-husband.'

'Jackson's a wonderful man. Yes, I know, why am I not still with him, then? That's life, I suppose.'

'Sorry, I didn't mean to raise the subject. I'm surprised I even mentioned another male human being while I've got a girl in my arms.'

Lucy sighed. 'Time's dragging.'

'Oh, thanks.'

'No, not because of you. I just wish I could take my mind off Carla until she comes back. Or until you go looking for her.'

Nathan laughed. 'There it is again, as if it's a given. Listen...' He cuddled her closer. 'I know a way to take your mind off things.'

'Oh, you mean one of Pyle's attractions? I forgot to tell you, he's got an indoor parachute wind tunnel somewhere.'

'No, not what I was thinking about.'

'What were you thinking of exactly?'

'Pyle's Love Maze.'

Lucy spluttered, 'Pyle's *what*!?'

'You've heard of Hampton Court maze? Well, this is a maze that shows you types of places where courting took place through the ages – you know, Roman, Victorian, Edwardian. When you turn a corner you find an arbor, or something, where you sit and... court.'

Lucy found that hysterically funny. He waited for her to calm down.

'Not a chance of that,' she told him.

'Is there not? Probably best I made it all up, then.'

'You cheater. There is that thing I almost told you about earlier on.'

'What thing?'

'You remember, we said we'd try it before we left here.'

'Oh, yeah.'

He was none the wiser, but he picked up his sandwich and followed her anyway.

Pringle, of course, fitted them out with their clothes, individually so they would not spoil the surprise, and they were taken by separate routes to the far northern reaches of Pyle's estate.

Nathan reached the huge aluminium hangar first, puzzled that it did not seem to fit in with the authentic Wild West gunslinger outfit of all black that he was wearing, with ornately stitched leather boots, red neckerchief and fantastically heavy Colt 45 in its holster, which he had played with continually, tied to his right leg.

Once inside, though, Nathan found an authentic western saloon, complete with glass-polishing bartender, bad piano player and cowboys playing cards around green-felt tables. There were other cowboys standing around looking menacing – Pyle not skimping on the Extras. Loving it all, Nathan moseyed to the bar, threw a silver dollar down and had the bartender pour out a shot of whiskey. He watched for it to overspill and burn the counter, as in *Back to the Future part III*, but it was just regular alcohol. He couldn't stop himself surreptitiously taking out his Colt again, just to have the feel of it – giggling quietly to himself like a little girl.

Lucy came in, causing Nathan to laugh out loud. She was made up like a tart, wearing a purplish taffeta dress with black lace at the top of the tight bodice. Her high black lace-up boots made her walk to him in a sexy manner, and, incidentally, the first thing she said to him was, 'I'm keeping these boots.'

'You look amazing. Not exactly what I expected.'

'What did you think they'd put me in?'

'Calamity Jane came to mind. Not a painted trollop.'

'I think I do painted trollop very well, thank you very much. Are you not getting me a drink?'

'They only gave me the one dollar.'

A drink appeared in front of Lucy. 'What's that?' she asked.

'That there looks like sarsaparilla.'

'Oh, lovely.'

Nathan had his gun out once more.

'You know what they say?' said Lucy, 'You're not supposed to take it out unless you intend to use it.'

'I bet you've said that line before.'

Nathan twirled the gun and then set it back in the holster.

'You haven't told me how great I look,' he said.

She tutted. 'You look brilliant.' She tried her drink, while perusing the room. 'Nathan, that man over there keeps staring at you.'

'I know. He's going to get it in a minute.'

'What's his problem?'

'I believe he thinks I stole his horse.'

'Did you steal his horse? Oh, he's starting to look very angry.'

'Maybe he's jealous of all the attention you're giving me.'

'He's coming closer.'

'Maybe he wants to take you upstairs.' She ignored that comment. He glanced round at the cowboy and did a mock sigh. 'I suppose I'd better take care of this. Make sure you stand well clear.'

Nathan turned to face up to the cowboy. Lucy backed away from the bar and everyone else ducked for cover. There followed a stand-off, both men assessing the other's capability, without any conversation. Nathan drew his gun and fired, shooting his slower opponent, who grasped at his stomach and slumped to the floor, firing his own gun loudly into the floorboards as he did so. The noise and smoke had been shocking. Lucy rushed back across to take hold of Nathan.

'Wow,' he said, seriously thrilled. 'How about that!? Hey, it's over now. Tell me I was fantastic.'

'You were fantastic.'

Nathan holstered his gun. Holding the "frightened" Lucy close, he watched his opponent being dragged from the saloon by his heels.

'Shall we go upstairs?' he asked Lucy.

The saloon returned to normal as if nothing had happened and the piano started up again.

'I thought you'd never ask,' she answered.

They mounted the stairs which turned left above the bar. There was just the one room which they entered; it was authentic too, down to the finest detail - brass bedstead, white porcelain wash basins, gaudy red curtains. Lucy sat on the bed and it squeaked. Nathan removed his gunbelt and draped it over the back of a chair.

'You took that off very reluctantly,' Lucy told him.

'Would you have minded if I'd kept it on?'

'Surprisingly... yes.'

Nathan sat beside her, making her bounce slightly. She smiled at him.

'Not quite Hammersmith,' he said.

'No, not quite Hammersmith.'

He fiddled with the tiny buttons at the neck of her dress.

'Would you like some help there, cowboy?'

'If you wouldn't mind.'

They kissed. Once her neck was free, he transferred his affections to her skin there.

TWENTY-ONE

Nathan and Lucy lay entwined in bed.

'You know what, Lucy? You were better second time round.'

'What do you mean by that? Are you suggesting you had me in a previous life?'

'Something like that. Hey, will I like living in Hammersmith?'

She giggled. 'Who says we're living together?'

'How can you bear to be apart from me after that?'

She snorted. 'You ain't all that, you know.'

'Tell me about Hammersmith.'

'What's to tell?'

'Have you got a view of the river?'

'A very poor one.'

'Did you know that bloke who swam out and stopped the Boat Race?'

'*No!!*'

They fell under the covers laughing.

***

The capsule closed on Nathan, as he went in search of Carla. Before the canopy turned opaque he gave the thumbs up to Pyle and Robinson, and blew a kiss towards Lucy. She caught it, then turned to smile at Jackson, who was close by to support her.

It was a turbulent journey for Nathan, bombarded with images of places and people, and with no feelings of elation. He was relieved to realise he was through to his destination, as light flooded across his closed eyelids. He opened his eyes, to see that again he was half in and half out of a supporting wall. Fear over Pyle's apparently flawed scientific genius engulfed him, imagining being stuck there forever and he swore under his breath for a long moment, before gathering his thoughts.

He looked from left to right but saw nobody about. Instead, he had a fabulous view through floor-to-ceiling glass out over a part of a city with a wide, busy river. He was high up in the building. Voices sounded in the office around a corner. 'American,' Nathan said to himself. He continued to listen. 'Of course, American - that's where Carla went.'

He tried not to become distressed at the thought that Carla was nearby but frustratingly out of view. Then the voices, happy and loud, came closer and a group of people in sharp business suits swamped past Nathan's face. He strained to see Carla as the people settled down in comfortable sofas to continue their discussions.

Nathan watched the woman who passed closest to him and was now sat at the nearest settee. He appraised her long blonde hair and sleek profile, under any other circumstances he would have been enjoying the sexy vision of her, before reminding himself that he should be seeing Carla.

'What the hell is this? Clearly I'm in the wrong fucking place.'

The blonde woman turned her head to the side. When she spoke, she did so without her associates noticing. 'Hello, Nathan.'

Nathan was stupefied. 'Carla, is that you?'

'In a way.'

'What do you mean?'

'I came out inside this person. She was standing beside my relative at the time. There's my relative over there, the woman with the really big hair.'

'Christ, Carla. Is that what's stopping you getting back? Everyone's worried about you back there.'

'Please, tell them not to be.'

'You tell them not to be. We'll get you back...'

152

'Nathan.'

'When I tell Pyle what's happened he'll do something...'

'Nathan. Nathan. I don't want to go back. Thank you for coming to get me, I love you for that, but I don't want to go back.'

'I beg your pardon?'

'Nathan, look at me. I'm in my twenties. I'm gorgeous for the first time in my life. I think I must be rich now. See the man by the window, the hunk over there? He just asked me out to lunch.'

Nathan was gobsmacked. 'But...'

'Nathan, really. It's okay. I don't feel like two people in one body. I don't think she minds having me. I want to go with this. I'm thrilled to bits.'

'Carla, I don't know what to say. But I don't think you've got much chance with the hunk.'

'Why's that?'

'He's just seen you talking to the wall.'

Carla flashed a look at the man but he seemed to be occupied in a conversation.

'He didn't really,' said Nathan. 'I wish you all the luck with him, and with this new life of yours.'

Carla smiled at him.

'Carla, you're quite a hottie, you know. Listen, I might only have a few minutes here left, assuming they manage to get me back at all. Let's not talk. We'll just keep looking at each other until I'm gone.'

'Okay, Nathan. I'll like that.'

Nathan and Carla exchanged a few more glances before he did in fact disappear.

Pyle and Dr Robinson helped Nathan from the capsule. The trip back had been even worse, and definitely his last one. Lucy stood nearby, relieved beyond measure. She shared a look with Nathan – it was all over now.

'I saw her,' Nathan told them all. 'I saw Carla.'

'What was her status?' asked Pyle, excited.

Nathan only had eyes for Lucy. 'She's well, she's happy; she's in someone else's body. She says she's staying where she is, thank you and good night.'

Nathan went over to Lucy, kissed her passionately, took her by the hand and led her out of the laboratory.

Pyle called after him, 'Nathan! Please explain. Nathan!? Nathan?'

***

Looking in, from outside the building, Carla and her colleagues continued their informal meeting. Carla smiled as the hunk came over to chat, perhaps to ask where she would like to go for lunch.

Looking in, from further away, they were sitting in the north tower of the World Trade Centre.

From further away still, an American Airways Boeing 767 swooped in low across the New York sky.

Genie-alogy